'I thought you

Elly pushed int
about ten minute

'As I was saying before you interrupted with
your late arrival—Sister Winthrop, isn't it?'
her adversary of the previous night continued
with malicious directness, 'I decided I'd better
introduce myself to all the staff as soon as
possible, so none of you mistake the new
owner of Gracemere for some big oaf poking
around the place for no valid reason.'

New owner! Elly shrank back into her seat.
Had she really called him a big oaf?

Dear Reader

In Caroline Anderson's ONCE MORE, WITH FEELING, Emily and David meet again after their divorce, in HEART ON THE LINE Jean Evans's Georgia goes to Ethiopia after a broken engagement, and in Australia Meredith Webber's Elly has A DIFFERENT DESTINY. We're very pleased to introduce new author Josie Metcalfe, whose Rebecca and Alex have NO ALTERNATIVE but to respond to each other. With such good reading, how could you not have a wonderful Christmas? Enjoy!

The Editor

!!!STOP PRESS!!! If you enjoy reading these medical books, have you ever thought of writing one? We are always looking for new writers for LOVE ON CALL, and want to hear from you. Send for the guidelines, with SAE, and start writing!

Having pursued many careers—from school-teaching to pig farming—with varying degrees of success and plenty of enjoyment, **Meredith Webber** seized on the arrival of a computer in her house as an excuse to turn to what had always been a secret urge—writing. As she had more doctors and nurses in the family than any other professional people, the medical romance seemed the way to go! Meredith lives on the Gold Coast of Queensland, with her husband and teenage son.

Recent titles by the same author:

WHISPER IN THE HEART
A TESTING TIME

A DIFFERENT DESTINY

BY

MEREDITH WEBBER

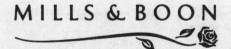

MILLS & BOON LIMITED
ETON HOUSE, 18-24 PARADISE ROAD
RICHMOND, SURREY TW9 1SR

*MILLS & BOON, the Rose Device and LOVE ON CALL
are trademarks of the publisher.*

*First published in Great Britain 1994
by Mills & Boon Limited*

© Meredith Webber 1994

*Australian copyright 1994   Philippine copyright 1994
This edition 1994*

ISBN 0 263 78886 5

*Set in Times 10 on 11 pt. by
Rowland Phototypesetting Limited
Bury St Edmunds, Suffolk*

03-9412-49983

Made and printed in Great Britain

CHAPTER ONE

ELLY watched the pretty young face suffuse with colour, and caught the sudden sheen of moisture in the young woman's soft brown eyes.

'At university they said. . .' the hapless nurse graduate bleated.

Now the wretched child is going to cry, Elly thought with a swift dart of pity, then pushed aside her sympathy. Like so many of the new graduates, Debbie Morrison had the potential to be an excellent nurse, but she would never succeed if she couldn't adapt to the pace of everyday routine on the wards.

'I think the university course for nursing is a great idea,' Elly told her firmly. 'It's just a shame the great brains who dreamed it up didn't follow through with more practical experience. You've been on another ward before you came to Neurovascular, so you must realise there are things you need to learn!'

She could hear her own exasperation—and the edge of tiredness snapping at the words! A particularly virulent strain of flu was sweeping through the nursing staff, and she was working overtime most days in an effort to help out. The preceptor who should be guiding Debbie was on the sick-list, which is why she, Elly, was here, at the end of a long, hard day, trying to drum some common sense into the young woman.

'What you are taught about patient management at university is quite correct, but you must get through all your duties each day. You have six patients to attend to, not just one or two!'

5

The tears were now streaming down and Debbie's face was a woebegone mess. Elly shifted uncomfortably, but hardened her heart against the despair.

'You have to learn to manage your time,' she insisted. 'Without that skill, you'll never make a good nurse, no matter how much you know about the theory! Now, off you go, and think about what I've said. I'll see you tomorrow.' Her voice was cold and emotionless. No matter how sympathetic she might feel towards the novice, it was her job to see that all the staff on the ward were educated in correct practices —a mistake by one of them not only reflected badly on her management, but could be fatal.

The weeping junior fled, leaving Elly in the small sitting-room, drained and exhausted. She gazed unseeingly out of the window, wondering for the thousandth time if she would ever adapt to this career that had been forced on her rather than chosen. She was an efficient and effective ward sister, but the satisfaction of regular hands-on nursing was missing, and in its place was a welter of paperwork, not to mention some distasteful, unpleasant duties like keeping staff on their toes.

'Does it give you a thrill of some kind, reducing kids like that to tears?'

The deep male voice was full of the anger she could not feel, and she spun around to face the intruder.

He filled the doorway, slightly hunched as if to diminish his size, his hands thrust deep into the pockets of an immaculate charcoal-grey suit. Inches taller than her own five feet ten, he was broadly built, with the wide shoulders and thick chest she associated with the concussed footballers who regularly graced the ward. Flecks of grey in his black hair and deep furrows on his brow probably made him look older than he really was, she decided, then wondered what on earth she was doing, summing up a total stranger in this way. And a belligerent stranger at that!

'I beg your pardon?' she muttered, realising too late that the words sounded more like an apology than the icy reproof she'd intended.

'It's that young girl you should be apologising to,' he said with an argumentative insistence, his voice grating across her nerves like sandpaper.

'I hardly think that's any of your business,' she replied with what she hoped was a calm, controlled indifference, although she could feel an unusual warmth in her cheeks, and a slow fuse of anger starting to burn in the deep recesses of her mind.

'Oh, no?' he said, the harsh tones now muted so the words had the silky feel of polished steel, and the subtle menace of an underlying threat.

'No!' she snapped, and tried to escape through the gap left as he leaned against the door-jamb of the small room that was used for interviewing patients and showing procedural videos.

'Ellen Winthrop, eh?' He read her name off her badge as she drew closer, and moved just enough to block off her retreat. Then his gaze slid over her in a searching, all-encompassing scrutiny that fanned the fitful anger into an almost overpowering rage. Whoever he was, he had no right treating her like an erring schoolgirl!

'Will you please stand aside and let me get on with my work?' She spat the words at him, her fury intensifying as she saw a half-smile tease at the corners of his lips. 'I don't know who you are, and I don't care, but what I do on my ward is my business and no one else's.'

'So the stories aren't entirely true,' he mused, as he

pushed himself off the door-jamb with a languid grace that struck Elly as strange in such a big man. 'There must be some blood there to produce such colour.'

'You're mad,' she muttered, and attempted again to pass him, but his hand shot out with surprising speed and clapped itself against her forehead, in the way a mother would feel for a temperature in a child.

'Definite warmth, as well!' he added as a clinical afterthought, before drawing aside to allow her to hurry away.

Gregor watched her go. He'd had the chief executive officer, who was in charge of the nursing staff, in his office all day, giving him details of the various wards, and the key staff who managed them. In her opinion, this was the most efficient sister in the hospital, but if she bought her success by trampling on the sensibilities of the nurses under her, then things would have to change.

He had his source of gossip as well, and remembered Debbie's fear when she knew Neurovascular was her next assignment! That was when he'd heard the 'ice-water in her veins' comment, and recalled ward sisters he'd encountered as a student who had been similarly labelled! He'd watch this one closely! He had his own, very definite ideas about how a hospital should be run.

Elly strode away from him, aware that her unprecedented haste was attracting sidelong glances from passing staff.

'You still here?'

The sister who had taken over from her an hour earlier looked up in surprise as Elly reached the desk that was the control centre for her ward. 'Get off home and grab some rest—tomorrow is sure to be worse,' she added cheerfully, and Elly was forced to smile.

Sue Childs had started with her at Gracemere five years ago, when the small private hospital had opened, and had remained through the birth of two children, switching to split shifts and night duty to accommodate the demands of motherhood with the needs of her work. She was as close a friend as Elly had, but they saw little of each other these days!

'My social life is non-existent!' The words followed her thoughts and burst from her lips with a rare resentment.

'You don't make much effort to improve it,' Sue told her drily, and the hot tension coiled inside Elly began to ease.

She chuckled quietly and shook her head. 'I didn't mean that kind of social life, Sue!' she remonstrated feebly. 'I was thinking how little we saw of each other apart from hello and goodbye at work!'

'Well, you will keep saying yes to extra duty. The roster clerk knows she's got a soft touch in you.'

Elly sighed and lifted her slim shoulders in resignation. 'It's easier for me to fill in for someone on the morning or evening split shifts.'

She didn't add, 'because I've no set commitments, no baby-sitter to find, no husband to consider,' but she thought the words, and they brought a rare sadness flooding through her.

'I can't understand it,' Sue said, pursuing her own train of thought. 'You're not unattractive, and you're good company. Bill would as soon talk to you as any of his male friends! He says you're soothing.'

'Well, thank you—and Bill—for that great compliment,' Elly mocked, dropping a slight curtsy. 'You make me sound like teething powder.'

'You OK?' Sue asked suddenly, peering intently at her.

Had she caught a hint of bitterness in the joking words?

'I'm fine, Sue, just tired!' Elly assured her with a wan smile, unable to explain, even to her best friend, a mood she could not understand herself. She gathered up a pile of paperwork she hadn't had time to look at during the day and said goodbye, her mind whirling in search of answers as she walked absentmindedly through the bustling hospital towards the stair-well that led down to the staff car park.

Having to speak firmly to a nurse was part of her duty, and one that, however much she disliked it, she accepted with the job. So, it couldn't have been the unavoidable interview with young Debbie that had shaken her composure and introduced a curious dissatisfaction into her calmly ordered life.

Surely it couldn't be that boorish fellow who'd upbraided her with such insolence? Whoever he was, he had no right speaking to her at all, so why should she care. Her feet slowed while she wondered about it.

Maybe he had a relative who was a patient, and his anxiety had found an outlet in his rudeness. Maybe his wife was ill. . . She did a mental check of the patients in Neurovascular and shook her head. No one fitted. There had been a suggestion of power in the man, not only in his build, but in an inexplicable impression of some inner core of strength.

That kind of man would have a beautiful, pampered wife—satin and lace négligés as against cotton nightdresses! she decided, then smiled grimly to herself, and tried to put the incident out of her mind. She was late enough already, without frittering away more precious time with unproductive thoughts. She resumed the smooth, swift gait that usually characterised her movement through the hospital, and shut her mind against unwanted intrusions.

At the bottom of the stairs, she set her shoulder against the heavy fire-rated glass door and shoved. The door swung outward, then stopped as it hit a heavy, slightly yielding obstruction.

There was a muttered curse from the shadowy darkness, but Elly had no time to consider who was skulking behind the door, for the papers she was holding had slipped from her hands, and were skittering across the car park at the whim of a capricious wind.

Securing the remnants of them against her chest with one arm, she dashed off in pursuit, only vaguely aware that the man she had shoved the door into was also helping. Grabbing the last she could see from the bonnet of a car, she turned, slightly breathless, to face her helper, her hand out to receive the papers he had gathered.

'Are these hospital papers?' he barked, and she recognised the voice, although his dark bulk had already given her a clue to his identity.

'Sort of,' she said, snatching at the crumpled sheets he held in a tightly clenched fist.

'Then why are they leaving the hospital?' he thundered, holding them up out of her reach. Elly took an involuntary step backwards, as if she feared a physical danger from so deep and dark a voice.

'Give me back those papers immediately,' she demanded, her voice quivering with an anger that was as unexpected as it was unfamiliar. 'And then get out of this car park before I call Security.'

'I think a call to Security might be a good idea,' he said softly, but she did not mistake the softness for any weakness. If anything, the threat in the words was made more implicit by the undertone. 'Surely it's against regulations to remove confidential papers from the premises?'

The words had an air of authority that jolted her, but she was not about to give up. Her free hand stretched out and punched the alarm button by the door.

'I don't know who you think you are,' she snapped, almost stamping her foot in frustrated indignation, 'but you've no right to be here in this car park, and I'll be delighted to watch Security throw you out.'

In spite of the dim light, she saw one curved eyebrow lift, and knew he was laughing at her. Ted Eames, their elderly night-watchman, appeared at the same time, and a sense of frustrated futility overwhelmed her. How could an old man like Ted throw anyone out—particularly a man built like a small tank?

Stiffening her spine, she smiled grimly at the new arrival, and had opened her mouth to demand he get rid of the intruder when she realised that Ted, ignoring her, had turned automatically to the big man, and was saying, in a placatory way, 'Is there something the matter, sir?'

'Ted, isn't it?' the man-mountain asked smoothly, and Elly nearly ground her teeth when she saw Ted's deferential nod. If he'd had a forelock he'd have tugged it, she decided bitterly.

'I've been checking on the lighting down here, and it seems a bit inadequate,' the deep voice continued. 'Perhaps you could draw up a plan for improving it, and we'll get the electrician to see if it's feasible.'

'Right you are, sir! Evening, Sister,' and the man was gone.

'I suppose you think you're funny,' Elly yelled, shaking with a rage she could not understand. 'I take it you're the new administrator, and find it more amusing to slink around spying on people instead of introducing yourself as any normal person would.'

The words spluttered as they flew from her lips, as if the only release for her feelings was the flow of invective. 'Well, you might have Ted Eames kow-towing to your lordship, but administrators have nothing to do with the nursing staff. I answer to the chief executive officer! Now give me those papers this instant or I'll. . .'

The fire petered out. What could she do? Calling Security hadn't helped, and the head of the nursing staff would be at home preparing dinner for her four riotous teenagers and accountant husband. The after-hours co-ordinator would be in her office, but she had the responsibility for the entire hospital and was always so busy it would be unfair to worry her at this time of the evening.

'That's got you floored, hasn't it,' he teased hatefully. 'Who exactly can you run to when you've been caught sneaking papers out of the hospital?'

He thought her pause was the product of guilt! Outraged by his sneering comment, she felt a reaction that needed a physical release. She wanted to hit out at the man, to thump and kick and pummel away at him, or jump up and down and scream in fury. What a pretty sight that would be, a small sane portion of her brain remarked, particularly if he *is* the new administrator.

She drew a long deep breath, and said in a voice that shook with the effort of restraint, 'Would you please give me back my papers? They are personal letters from patients or their relations that I don't have time to answer while I am on duty, and——'

'Doesn't the ward clerk do that sort of thing?' he demanded, looking suspiciously at the papers he still held clutched in his big fist, then peering at her with the distasteful misgiving of a diner who had found a small insect on his lettuce.

'She types all the business letters I send out, replies to GPs about their patients, notes about medications to people who've been released, but. . .'

Why on earth am I telling him all of this? she wondered, trying desperately to regain the characteristic reserve that was her defence against the irritations of her job.

'I'd like to check them,' he said coldly, obviously disbelieving every word she said, 'and I'd like the lot.' He moved his free hand as if to seize the bundle she still clasped to her chest.

All the unfamiliar anger had dissipated, and in its place was a dragging tiredness. Her shoulders drooped defeatedly, but she still refused to give way.

'I can't hand over these papers to you,' she said, wearily shaking her head. 'Even with proof that you are in administration here, I doubt that they are within your jurisdiction.'

'Lost all your fight rather suddenly, didn't you!' he mocked, fanning the dying embers of anger back to sparking life.

'It just so happens that I have been on duty in this place for nearly twelve hours.' She bit the words out from between clenched teeth. 'I am cold and tired and hungry and I want to get home. I do not appreciate having total strangers upbraiding me for doing what I consider to be my job, nor do I need pointless arguments in the car park with a great big stupid oaf who's trying to assert his extremely dubious authority. Now give me back those papers or I'll go straight inside to the after-hours co-ordinator and report you for harassment.'

He reached out so suddenly that she flinched away, staggering slightly as one foot slipped off the concrete pad that lead out into the car park, but his arm snaked beyond her to press the security button once again, then grasped at her elbow, steadying her against her will.

'If you've been on duty for that length of time, the last thing you need is more work to do at home,' he said, giving her a little shake to underscore the words. 'No wonder you were giving that young nurse such a hard time—no one can operate effectively when they're overtired.'

'I can't believe my ears,' she snorted, twitching away from the large warm hand that was intruding so forcefully into her personal space. 'Now you're making excuses for me!'

She glared up into his face, noticing, now her eyes had adjusted to the gloom, that the dark eyes were a kind of grey colour, not the brown she had imagined. 'What I do is none of your business!'

She paused between each word, spacing them out to provide an emphasis that even a two-year-old should understand.

'Was there something else, sir?'

Ted had reappeared, looking like a garden gnome beside the tall intruder.

'Yes, Ted. I'd like you to take these papers up to. . .' He paused for a moment, and Elly held her breath. She did not want to continue her battle of wills with this man in front of Ted, but she would defend the innocuous papers from him with all her might.

'Take them back up to Neurovascular. Sister has had too long a day to be taking extra work home!'

Elly hoped her jaw did not actually drop, although it wouldn't have surprised her to find it had. The man had swept away any argument she might be able to advance with one masterly stroke. The bitter taste of defeat was as real as bile against her tongue.

'All the papers, Sister,' he continued implacably, holding out a patient hand for the untidy bundle she still held.

With a weak nod of acknowledgement for this winning move, she pushed them towards Ted, then spun away from the two men, and walked towards her car, holding her head high so the stranger would not guess the pain and humiliation searing through her body.

She drove through the quiet streets with a tense concentration that was as foreign to her as the anger had been. The man had upset her equilibrium, and somehow the two chance encounters had disturbed more than her temper. Normally, however tired she was, she headed home with a sense of satisfaction—a feeling of contentment with her job, and the work she'd achieved within its confines.

Bleak was the only way to describe her mood tonight, she decided, turning off the wide road into the side street that led down towards the Broadwater, and the quiet road that ran along its fringing park.

Home was a two-storeyed fibro house, originally built as a weekend beach house for her parents and two older brothers. Her father's retirement, soon after her arrival—an unexpected change-of-life baby for her mother—meant that it was the only home she could remember, just as the tall elderly man who had spent his days fishing in the sparkling waters opposite the house, or reading and writing in the big book-lined study, was the only father she had ever known, although scrapbooks and photographs showed a handsome, red-haired young man posing on the strip of white sand, and a laughing young father sailing with his sons.

She had his red hair, and the pale, sun-sensitive skin that went with it! She had his height, and, presumably, his dedication to work, for he had continued with his research and theorising long after his retirement.

She pulled up into the drive with a sigh. She also had him! But the man who had been a giant in his time, whose words and works on the functioning of the brain and central nervous system were still used as a basis for study today, had slipped into a world where none could reach him, greeting people with an unfailing courtesy, but not recognising who they were, or understanding the words they spoke to him.

She sighed again and climbed out of the car, walking forward to greet Mrs Hobson, who stood in the brightly lit downstairs doorway with a slightly anxious look on her face.

'Sorry I'm so late,' she muttered, not wanting to talk, nor to have to explain. 'Dad OK?'

'He's fine. We've had a lovely day!' the older woman replied, and Elly uttered, not for the first time, a silent prayer of thanks to the fate that had led the Hobsons to her door when she began her search for a kindly couple who would care for her father. 'But you're working too hard. You'll get that flu yourself if you're not careful!'

Elly smiled at her and shook her head.

'I'm tough,' she said with a smile. 'You ask any of the junior nurses at Gracemere, and they'll assure you that no germ, bug, virus or bacteria would dare to attack Old Winnie!'

'They've no right to talk so disrespectful,' Mrs Hobson tutted, and would have launched into her 'I don't know what the world is coming to' speech if Elly hadn't hastened to intervene.

'I'll just look in on Dad, then go on upstairs and have an early night. It *has* been a long day.'

Mrs Hobson stepped aside, and she went through into the warm, bright flat she'd renovated and furnished with such loving care when she had realised her father was deteriorating rapidly. The walls of the sitting-room were lined with shelves, and the books he'd loved so much were stacked ceiling high. To the left was his bedroom, looking out over the stretch of water that had given him such pleasure, and across to South Stradbroke, the island where they'd camped together on fishing trips when the tailor were running in the wild surf.

He was in bed, but not asleep, and she walked over to take his hand and bent to kiss his thick white hair. Settling into the chair beside him, she told him about her day, the patients and their operations, the visitors, the medical staff, pouring out words he only half understood. She would have liked to tell him about the arrogant stranger, to use speech in an effort to probe her own distracting anger towards the man, but she'd realised a long time ago that he could sense distress in her voice, and would become disturbed and restless himself.

'It's passed my dinnertime and I'm starving,' she said at last, squeezing his fingers in a silent farewell. 'I'll come in to see you in the morning before I leave for work, if I'm not called up for the six o'clock shift again.'

With a wave to the Hobsons, who were enthralled by one of their favourite quiz programmes on the television, she walked back to the hall and up the internal staircase that lead to her part of the old house.

Franny, the blue point Siamese who deigned to share her life, looked scornfully at her through narrowed slits of blueness, as if to say, See if I care that you're late!

'And you're another symbol of something I don't want to admit,' Elly told her crossly, nudging at the animal with one foot as it insinuated itself between her ankles 'Typical old maid, coming home alone each night to her elderly father and spoilt, demanding cat! You're part of a metaphor, that's all!'

She opened the tin of cat food before peering into the refrigerator, to see what delectable treat she didn't feel like cooking for her solitary meal tonight.

'Damn him!' she said to the cat as she shut the refrigerator door with unnecessary force. Franny looked up with a widening of her imperturbable eyes, then bent her head and continued eating her dinner.

Deciding that salmon on toast and a hot cup of tea was all she could manage, Elly fixed the snack then carried it on a tray across to the big chair by the glass windows, that enclosed the wide front veranda of the house. Curling comfortably into the old softness, she stared out through the Norfolk pines to the waters beyond, calm and mysterious, silvered to a mirrored finish by a half-moon, so that no hint of their hidden life or secret depths could be seen from above.

Like people, I suppose, she decided, sipping at the tea. What you see is not always what you get!

The fleeting fancy only fuelled her disquiet, and she shifted irritably in the chair, annoyed that the peace and tranquillity of her home was also disturbed by her strange mood of dissatisfaction. It couldn't have been the man who'd caused it! It must have been the long day, or the realisation that she had little time to catch up with friends like Sue, despite the fact that nothing vital or exciting was happening in her life outside work!

Or was it her contact with Debbie? Did the young nurse graduate remind her too strongly that she was getting old? Was twenty-eight old? Certainly it was a long time since anyone had asked her for a date, and longer still, she admitted, with a rueful smile at the cat which had leapt up on to her knee, since she'd accepted such an invitation.

Coming to terms with her father's degeneration had taken a long time. At first she had protected him from added stress by keeping to familiar routines, which meant encouraging his friends to drop in but restricting his contacts with new people. Then, as his friends found less reward and more discomfort in their visits, these had stopped. The social contact had virtually ceased, and she and the Hobsons became his only links with the outside world.

Unnoticed, and therefore unquestioned, the few invitations she had been used to receiving had dried up, and she sought and found a satisfaction in the new life she forged for herself. Until today!

'I'll be weeping into your fur if I don't snap out of this,' she told Franny, pushing her off on to the floor as the phone jangled its summons.

'Ted Eames brought in that pile of book-work you were taking home,' Sue explained. 'I thought you might have left it on top of your car and driven off, and rang to let you know it's safe.'

'Thanks, Sue! I knew Ted had it. It was only letters from grateful patients I wanted to reply to tonight——'

'And about three pages of figures that you must have picked up with the letters. What would our chief exec think if you were caught smuggling that valuable information out of the place?' Sue teased, laughing, as they all did, about Sally Jeffs, their security-conscious head of the nursing staff.

But Elly couldn't laugh. A deadly coldness crept through her bones as she remembered the fistful of paper the man had held. The car park was poorly lit; she had written a memo to complain about it herself. Had they been standing in a shaft of light thrown from the stair well? It had been bright enough for her to see the colour of his eyes, she remembered. Would the aggravating stranger have been able to tell the difference between written and numbered notes?

'Figures?' she repeated weakly.

'Looks like dosages or something—definitely your writing,' Sue said cheerfully, unaware of the tumult she was causing in her friend's solar plexus.

'It's work I was doing on the patient-controlled analgesic,' she muttered, knowing that she'd spoken to the chief exec about the paper she was writing, but unable to remember if she'd obtained her permission to take copies of the records out of the hospital.

'Don't sound so despairing,' Sue joked. 'It's all safe and sound. Just be thankful it was Ted who picked them up, not some young nurse who wanted to make trouble for you.'

The trouble a young nurse could make was nothing compared to the strife the new administrator could cause if he had seen the figures, she worried, as she said goodbye to Sue and wondered about the possibility of finding another job as satisfying and convenient.

That's nonsense, she admonished herself, clearing up the kitchen. You are a good nurse, doing a job you enjoy, and normally you don't see the administrator more than once or twice a month, and then only in passing. Stop panicking, she ordered firmly, but the brave words were not backed up with any conviction, as her heart quailed with an uncertainty that was so foreign it frightened her.

CHAPTER TWO

As ELLY turned into the familiar car park an hour before she was due to go on duty, the strange niggling disquiet that had affected her the previous evening surfaced again. Perhaps it was time for a change! She shrugged away the traitorous idea with a fatalistic acceptance. There'd be no change at the moment, no trips away, no working holidays abroad, nor any of the exciting challenges she'd envisaged for herself when she'd been younger.

'I've some paperwork to catch up on,' she explained to the sister on the split shift who had charge of her ward at this hour. 'I'll take it into the interview room to keep out of your way.'

With a hammering heart, she grabbed the slightly crumpled papers and hurried off, not daring to look until she was shut into the little room. The pages of figures were there, as Sue had said, but she recognised at once that they were her own calculations and not copies of hospital documents accidentally caught up in the pile. Setting them aside to file in the special folder reserved for the research paper she was preparing, she started on the letters, writing a personal note to all the people kind enough to express their appreciation of the service they had received in her ward.

To Elly, this was the greatest reward of her job, and, although she knew she was criticised by some colleagues for her strict approach to all aspects of patient care, and for being hard on the nurses under her if they failed in any aspect of it, she also knew that her determination paid off in many ways, and these letters were part of the proof.

She had finished five replies before there was a light tap on the door and the departing sister popped her head through the gap. 'I'll be off soon. Nothing you should know about overnight, and all your charges seem bright and positive this morning. There's a memo from the chief exec about meetings scheduled throughout the day. You're down for the first at ten a.m.'

Regular staff meetings were held fortnightly, but it was unusual to get through a week without something cropping up that necessitated an extra briefing. Changes to Health Department regulations and rulings were the most common excuse for an additional, and to Elly unnecessarily time-consuming gathering. She sighed, accepting the inevitable, while her mind ran through the expected dramas of the day.

'I'll come and check the cupboard with you before you leave,' was all she said, realising the other woman was in a hurry to get away.

Checking the dangerous drugs when staff changed duty was a ritual never to be missed, and she walked through to the pantry where the double-locked safe was kept with a smug feeling of self-congratulation that 'her' ward had such a good record in this regard. It was the normal start to every shift, like a signal of some kind that switched on the activities of the day. The tally of drugs dispensed corresponded with what remained, and she said goodbye to the split shift sister and returned the key of the cabinet to the desk.

Day staff flitted through the corridors, most on duty early, intent on greeting their patients and getting started on the day's routine. As always, there was a sense of urgency as if they each fought a private battle to finish their duties before some crisis intervened to throw the system out of kilter.

Elly was reading the admissions list for the day when she saw the light come on above the door in Room Seven. As she stepped through the open end of the U-shaped desk, she glimpsed a tall, now-familiar figure approaching down the main corridor, with Debbie Morrison moving confidingly close to his side, her pretty dark head tilted upwards as she obviously hung on his words.

There was an ease between them that suggested more than a casual meeting, and something about the association filled Elly with a vague disquiet.

'You're late, Nurse Morrison,' she said, the words snapping out automatically as she hurried past the pair. Five minutes, that's all, she acknowledged to herself. Would she have said anything if the man had not been by her side?

Entering Room Seven, she was surprised to see one of her most reliable nurses over by the window of the room, examining a dressing with a look of concern on her face.

'Morning, Mr Stevens,' she said brightly, then added a quick, 'May I see you for a moment, Nurse,' before retreating backwards out of the room.

'I'm sorry, Sister,' the girl said as she came into the corridor, the offending dressing on top of a small stainless steel dish. 'I hope Mr Stevens didn't notice, but I was so shocked when I saw it I hit the button, then went across to the light to have a better look.'

Elly reached out for the dish, and lead the way back to the scrub room, listening as the nurse continued her explanation.

'I always look for a leak of cerebro-spinal fluid when I change laminectomy dressings, but, somehow I never expect to find it. I know I shouldn't have reacted in front of the patient, but it was such a shock!'

'If it is what it seems to be from that halo effect, the patient will have to know,' Elly reassured her, pleased that the nurse had at least realised what she had done wrong, and knowing she'd be unlikely to do it again. 'You get a runner from Pathology down here. They can test the fluid. Dr Collins is Mr Stevens' surgeon, and he'll be in any minute for a ward round. If there's a dural tear, he may decide to open up the wound and stitch it or do an epidural blood patch.'

'Poor Mr Stevens,' the nurse responded, as they both walked back to the desk. 'He was so certain he'd be ready to stand up and move a little today.'

It was a typical, fiddly interruption to the day's routine. The surgeon decided to have a closer look which meant the patient had to be prepared and sent back to Theatre at a time when the other pre-op patients were due to be prepped. Theatre lists were changed to accommodate the shift in priorities, and the timing of pre-med injections altered accordingly.

'I thought you had a meeting at ten,' the ward clerk reminded Elly, as she finally slumped into her chair behind the desk at a few minutes past.

'Oh, hell,' she muttered inelegantly, but straightened her cap and rose to her feet, hurrying off towards the administration rooms with a hasty, 'You know where to find me,' flung back over her shoulder.

She pushed into the small meeting room about ten minutes late, attracting a steely glare from the interfering stranger who was on his feet in front of an enthralled audience.

'As I was saying before you interrupted with your late arrival—Sister Winthrop, isn't it?——' her adversary of the previous evening continued with malicious directness, 'I decided I'd better introduce myself to all the staff as soon as possible, so none of you mistakes the new owner of Gracemere for some big oaf poking around the place for no valid reason.'

New owner! Elly shrank back into her seat as a polite titter of laughter at what they perceived to be a joke relaxed the audience. Had she really called him a big oaf? She seemed to recall she might have, and he had certainly looked directly at her when he said the words.

'As a trained specialist, I had often wondered why so many private hospitals are owned and run by non-medical companies and individuals. I realise they have business skills most doctors never acquire, but I am reasonably certain that, with a good administration, I will succeed in keeping up the high standards already set here, and maybe contributing some ideas of my own.'

A muted buzz ran round the room, fired by an underlying excitement as the senior nursing staff realised the possible advantages in having a trained medico in charge of the complex.

Would the advantages outweigh the disadvantage of having to work for a man like this? Elly wondered. She looked back up at him trying to read something in his impassive face. She knew from experience that there was an anger in the man, leashed at present, but ready to explode from just beneath the surface any time.

There was something in the way he stood—a kind of easy slouch, hands in pockets, shoulders hunched slightly forward—that made her wonder about his commitment to the hospital. About his commitment to anything?

Was he disillusioned with the practice of his profession? Was that what had caused the anger? Or disappointed with more worldly considerations? she wondered cynically. After all, here was a man who'd given up working with people, presumably because the financial rewards of owning a hospital were much greater.

It needn't worry you, she assured herself, as dismay spread through her. It will be in his interest to maintain the high standard of care provided at the hospital, and how often did you see the previous owners anyway? But, as she listened half-heartedly to the rest of what amounted to a pep talk, no silent assurances could banish the feeling of unease that plucked at her nerves.

The chief executive thanked him kindly, not by name, which would have been helpful for the late-comers, Elly thought, and the man strode down the aisle to the door at the back of the room.

'I'd like to see you when you finish for the day, Sister Winthrop,' he said quietly as he passed, and Elly felt a deep flush sweeping up her throat and into her face, flooding it with colour.

How dared he treat her like this! Exactly like an unruly student being put on the mat for lateness, she realised, with a bitterness that was so rare it shocked her.

Amy Godwin, the sister in charge of the acute medical ward caught up with her as she hurried out, saying excitedly, 'Isn't he great? Wonder if he's married? He looks quite old, doesn't he?'

Elly had to smile. It was well known that Amy's ambition was to marry a doctor, although Steve Barnett, the kind and caring male sister who ran the theatres like a well-oiled machine, was hopelessly in love with her and courted her with a patient persistence.

'I don't care about his age or marital status,' Elly

told her as they parted to go back to their wards, 'just as long as he keeps his hands off Neurovascular. It's taken me five years to get it running as smoothly as it does, and I don't need any changes!'

The familiar 'Who's got the key?' cry was ringing down the passageway when she returned, and she was pleased to see Debbie Morrison respond, snatching it up from the desk, and heading towards the drug cupboard with the controlled swiftness that was the natural movement of a good nurse. Maybe she'd dried her tears last night, then considered what Elly had been saying. Something had smartened her footwork!

'You've a new patient, Kathryn Wilson, coming in later, Debbie,' she said when the young woman returned the key to the desk. 'As your preceptor is still off sick, I'll sit in for the admission then explain the procedure for you if you like.'

She watched the pretty face break into a relieved smile.

'I'd be so grateful,' Debbie told her quickly. 'I have looked it all up, but with an acoustic neuroma, and the possibility that the patient might lose her hearing, I was worried about how much to say.'

'Her doctor should have prepared her for it,' Elly replied calmly, hiding the very real pleasure she experienced when she realised the girl had done her homework and had been thinking through all the possible ramifications of the operation. Instinct had told her Debbie would eventually make a good nurse, and this was a small particle of proof.

'The fact that a neuro-surgeon is performing the operation means they think there might be a slim hope of saving her hearing in that ear. You'll find an ear, nose and throat man will do the operation and go in from a cut behind the external ear, if the MRI shows the acoustic nerve is already badly damaged. This usually provides more protection for the facial nerve but destroys the cochlear and semicircular canals.'

She watched the girl's face and knew she understood, but a dismayed expression dulled the youthful beauty as she said soberly, 'I read through her background. She's only twenty, and a car accident when she was a child has already left her deaf in the other ear.'

Elly caught the anguish in the tone, but only said bracingly, 'The surgeon will do what he can, Nurse, but he can't perform miracles. Give me a call when she gets here.'

She watched Debbie walk away, and remembered herself at a slightly younger age, railing against the fates that could destroy the harmonious life of a patient in a split second of trauma, or plant the insidious growth of a silent menace within an outwardly healthy body. She hoped Debbie would learn, as she had, to hide the anger and the pity from the patients, treating them all with the confident serenity that was the hallmark of a good nurse.

Kathryn Wilson was late—so late both she and Debbie should have been off-duty—but neither of them was willing to leave until they had spoken to the young woman who would be their responsibility after she returned from Intensive Care in a few days.

When she did arrive, they were surprised. She was beautiful, in an ethereal way that made her seem much younger than her twenty years. Slight, and blonde, and obviously nervous, she turned repeatedly to a patient, grey-haired woman who was introduced as her mother.

Debbie ran them through the admission forms with an easy charm, then turned to Elly, who asked, 'Has your surgeon explained the operation?'

'Yes, he has,' Mrs Wilson replied doubtfully, while Kathryn continued to look scared.

'Do you want to ask anything about it?' Elly persisted, feeling that there was something wrong.

'He said I could lose my hearing in that ear,' Kathryn said loudly, and Elly realised she had already lost a lot of it. 'I'll be deaf and my face will be different!'

The despair behind the words tore at Elly's heart, and she saw Debbie blinking quickly.

'You may not be,' Elly told her. 'Do you know what happens?'

Kathryn looked stubbornly back at her, then shook her head.

'I couldn't understand it, really,' she admitted.

'I'll try to show you,' Elly offered, knowing that more detailed explanations could often help to allay fears. She picked up the little whiteboard she used to draw her sketches, and quickly mapped out a spidery mass of nerves, marring the symmetry of the lines with a blob across them.

Looking directly at Kathryn, she spoke clearly and carefully.

'The nerves are like cobwebs, fine and sticky. They twine around themselves. The tumour is like chewing gum, caught in and around the fibres, so you can guess how tricky it is to get out. If it is left there, it will grow and eventually cause other damage, and possibly even death by pressing on the brain stem and all the nerves that have their roots there.'

She sketched in the paths of the nerves, then watched as the new patient absorbed what she had said, and nodded her understanding.

'The acoustic nerve is the eighth cranial nerve, and runs close to the seventh, which is the facial. Sometimes, in removing all of the tumour there is damage to the facial nerve, which results in some paralysis on one side of the face. It may not happen, Kathryn,' she added, 'but, if it does, it can often be partially corrected later with plastic surgery.'

'I can see why it's so hard to tell beforehand,' the girl said at last, studying the rough sketch with interest, and Elly smiled at her.

'You have a top surgeon, and he'll do everything in his power to save your hearing and your facial nerve.'

'And we'll be here to look after you when you come back to the ward,' Debbie said, with a smile that hid her own misery.

'But what if I am deaf after it?' Kathryn asked.

'Then we will help you all we can and so will the doctors and therapists and your family. You will learn to adapt and to live with it. Many things will change for you, but it won't be an end of everything, Kathryn, just a new beginning.' Elly smiled encouragingly, although her own heart was heavy with pity.

'A new beginning?' she wavered.

'Of course! And it could start right now. Instead of thinking "why me?" and panicking, try to think about all the things you do every day, and how being deaf will change these if it happens. Then you work out ways to cope with the changes, and things you can do to make allowances for your deafness. That way you'll be more prepared, and have something definite to focus on as you recuperate, *if* the worst happens and the nerve is damaged.'

The charged atmosphere eased as if some fears had been diminished, and the four of them sat and talked, all contributing ideas that might help Kathryn to adapt, should the worst occur.

'I'll take you to your room and introduce you to the nurse who'll be looking after you this evening,' Debbie said at last, and led Kathryn and her mother away.

Elly hurried back to her desk, anxious to tidy up and get away.

'Did you have your personal audience with the new boss?' Sue asked, as she appeared, and she remembered his summons with a feeling of horror. It was an hour since she was due to finish. Would he know that? Would he still be at the hospital?

She was about to dash away when she saw Debbie emerge from Kathryn Wilson's room, the tears she could no longer control streaming down her cheeks.

There were times for being tough and unemotional in her situation, but this was not one of them. She slipped a comforting arm around the girl's shoulders and led her back to the interview-room.

'She's younger than I am,' Debbie sobbed, while Elly patted her and listened to the flow of words that would help ease her distress. 'Being deaf will mean she's totally cut off from the world! It would be like being dead inside!'

'Exactly like that for a while,' Elly agreed, hoping her quiet, measured tone would replace some of Debbie's shaken confidence. 'That's why we must do all we can to help her; to draw her back into the world with signs and signals, writing messages, making sure we all look at her as we speak, and mime what we want at the same time. We must try to keep our sentences as simple as possible, and ask questions that she can answer with a yes or no. I have an excellent book about nursing deaf patients. If you'd like to read it, I'll bring it in tomorrow. Kathryn will be in Intensive Care for a few days after the operation, so you'll have time to skip through it before she comes back to you.'

'I'd love to read it,' the nurse replied, moving away

from Elly's sheltering arm to give her a watery smile. 'Thank you for understanding!'

'You get off home now,' Elly chided, anxious to get things back on a professional footing. 'Working overtime on a regular basis is no good for any of my nurses.'

With another strained smile, Debbie left, blowing her nose, and mopping at her tear-stained face as she went out through the door. Elly watched, a smile hovering on her lips as she realised how much she liked the young nurse and her caring attitude.

It was like a replay of the previous evening, for the new owner materialised in the space vacated by Debbie, a frown drawing his black eyebrows together like a bar of wrath across his face.

'So you do get pleasure from other's tears,' he uttered, misreading her smile.

Elly stepped backwards, as if to escape a force she could not overcome.

'Well?' he barked into a silence that had gone on for so long it seemed to crush against her nerves.

'I was coming to see you now,' she said, ignoring his anger and trying to sound like the coolly efficient ward sister she knew herself to be. 'We had a late admission, and needed to spend some time with her.'

'Do you always attend to admission procedures yourself, or was it simply a way of putting off your appointment with me?' he demanded abrasively, firing once again the surge of quick temper that Elly thought she had conquered years ago.

'This was a twenty-year-old girl who is likely to wake up deaf. If I'd thought Ted Eames or Santa Claus could help allay her fears, I'd have had them here as well. There are no hard and fast rules in nursing, whatever you may think, Mr—Dr—Whoever-you-are, and, if you're into time-and-motion studies,' she added bitterly, 'then you should have invested your money into something that dealt with machines, not people.'

She glared at him, her fists clenched at her sides, and her head drawn up high on her rigid frame, unaware that her fury had lit her cheeks to a deep rose-pink, and added a glittering spark to her pale green eyes.

Gregor Ballantyne was taken aback. He forgot the wrath he'd felt when he saw Debbie's tear-streaked face. For some reason or other he was thinking of the Valkyrie, or was it the sea nymph, Siren, he meant? He could see 'Old Winnie' as he knew the staff irreverently called her, clad in flowing greenery, that bright hair unleashed around her head like fantastic seaweed, luring poor sailors into hidden dangers.

'I know a little more about hospitals than I do about factories,' he pointed out, then wondered why he was almost apologising to this infuriating woman.

'Then you'll know that being late for appointments is an occupational hazard,' she said dryly, and he was obscurely pleased to see her hands unclench and her stiff shoulders relax. 'We had a laminectomy patient with a CSF leak this morning, who had to be taken back to Theatre. I could, of course, have left him in the ward until after I'd attended your welcome address, but my priorities have always been the patients!'

He couldn't miss the sarcasm! Damn the woman, did she think he'd called her to his office to rebuke her? Was she trying to put him in the wrong?

'I do understand how easily a schedule can be shot to pieces,' he said stiffly. 'I wanted to speak to you about something quite different.'

He paused, uncertain now how to approach this prickly, defensive creature who apparently resented his very existence. Was she a man-hater? Did such women actually exist? He remembered his university days, when he and other male students had crept around the big public teaching hospital, forever in awe of the ramrod-stiff matron—reputed to feed on male students!

'Well, here I am!' Elly prompted impatiently, as the man appeared to have lapsed into a coma. Her stomach was reminding her that lunch had been a quick cup of coffee and she was afraid the growling protests would soon be audible. 'No doubt it's about the papers leaving the hospital last night. I can explain those, as well,' she added crossly.

Was she so tough on her staff that she assumed any conversation must be about shortcomings? They'd started off badly, but he would prefer to make peace with the woman, if only because staff changes at this stage could be disruptive.

'I realise you're already late getting away from this place, but can you spare the time for a cup of coffee in my office?' he asked in a placatory tone that made her raise her eyebrows in astonishment. He had done nothing but berate her since they met, and now was actually inviting her to join him in a cup of coffee! 'The chief exec told me about about the research work you're doing, and I would like to discuss it with you, but, of course, I could make some other time,' he explained.

Had he seen the figures and spoken to Sally? He sounded almost humble, Elly thought, but a quick look at his face reminded her that there was more to this man than was apparent in the smooth talk and harsh good looks. There were some shadows beneath that sternly handsome mask—anger for one thing, and something else that she couldn't quite define. Yet, in spite of her uncertainty about the new power in the hospital, the opportunity to talk to someone about her work was irresistible.

'Can you give me a few moments to make a phone call and grab a sandwich from the canteen?' she asked hesitantly.

He nodded, then said abruptly, 'Make your phone call, but I'll arrange the sandwiches. Shall we say ten minutes?'

Who did she have to ring? he wondered. He knew she was unmarried, but she could easily have a live-in lover, in spite of the hospital gossip that wrote her off as the typical 'spinster'. She was a plain woman but he imagined she could be quite striking if dressed correctly. His mind took her out of the white uniform that did nothing for her brilliant hair colouring and seemed to drain the colour from her face, then redressed her in dark blue, before he closed off his meandering thought-waves with an abrupt shake of his head.

Why should he be concerned about who—or was it whom?—she rang. After Jocee had walked out, he'd sworn off women for life! Sworn off 'relationships' at any rate! Better to play it cool, dating women who understood the rules of the game, choosing a sophisticated beauty when the circumstances demanded he have a decorative female on his arm and remaining unentangled. Decorative was the operative word! Nothing like the tall, pale tyrant who ruled her little empire with such fierce authority she reduced her staff to tears.

And the staff at Gracemere were definitely off-limits! Mixing work and pleasure was not a recipe for success. Then, having proclaimed this loudly in his mind, he wondered. Perhaps, if Jocee had been a nurse—if she'd understood just a little of the pressures of his work. . .? But that was all in the past, he reminded himself bitterly. Like so much else!

If only she'd stuck around until he'd had to leave the work he'd loved, and bought into the hospital as a way of keeping in touch! Would a job that could easily be restrained within the nine-to-five boundaries have satisfied her?

His freewheeling thoughts came to an abrupt halt at the door of his office, and he went through to phone the kitchen and order some fresh sandwiches and a pot of coffee. Nine-to-five? Who was he kidding? It was closer to seven already!

He called 'Come in,' in response to the light tap on the door, and watched with a strange pleasure as Sister Ellen Winthrop glided through into his office. She moved with a grace that was rare in such a tall woman, and he was obscurely pleased to see that, although she'd removed her cap and probably tried to straighten the fine strands of hair that escaped the tight braid to cluster round her face, she had not put on new lipstick, or obviously tried to improve her appearance before facing the new man in the hospital.

Business was business with this woman!

The coffee and sandwiches arrived with an orderly, and he gestured for her to help herself, while he poured the coffee and put the cup within her reach, pushing the sugar and milk to the side of the desk near where she sat.

'I've seen articles on research which trialed the use of patient-controlled analgesics in the treatment of cancer,' he began, while she tucked into the sandwiches with a healthy enjoyment, 'but not seen any figures related to patients in post-operative situations.'

She pushed a folder across the desk towards him.

'It was the successful figures in the cancer studies that prompted me to persuade the hospital to try it out in Neurovascular,' she told him, pausing from her demolition of the snack for long enough to explain. 'Drug usage in my ward is the highest in the hospital, mainly because of the high turnover of patients and the post-operative pain, so it was the feasible place to attempt a clinically controlled trial.'

He was perusing her work as he listened, but now looked up at her, the papers forgotten. 'You're actually trialing it with some patients on the patient control and others not?'

He was astounded that any person would generate so much extra work for herself.

She nodded, finishing a mouthful and chasing it down with a quick gulp of coffee.

'But it's hard to balance it scientifically,' she told him. 'In letting patients choose between the patient-control and staff-administered, you cut out a blind selection of patients, which could produce questions about the validity of the results.'

She looked up at him for a moment, her eyes seeming to bore into his brain, as if to check that he was actually taking in what she was saying. The quick comprehensive assessment reminded him of something, but she was speaking again, and he had to concentrate on the words.

'It may be that patients who choose to control their own analgesic have a different pain threshold or a more positive attitude to their recovery phase, or one of a hundred other psychological boosters that limit their need for pain relief.'

He was startled by the unmistakable commitment in her suddenly sparkling eyes and the tight edge of excitement in her beautifully modulated voice. The enthusiasm, catching him unaware, carried him along, although his decision to see her about the research had been based more on good business sense than any particular interest in the project. 'So you are finding that drug usage is down in the patients who opt for self-regulation?'

'By about twenty per cent,' she agreed happily, so absorbed by the work she was explaining that her cool, defensive reserve had vanished. 'It also seems that they can come off the stronger drugs much more quickly so we have less risk of addiction, and a faster recovery phase because there are less side-effects of strong medications. I try not to get overly excited about it, because the sample is still so small—less than a hundred patients so far. . .'

Something of the joy of the challenge that was evident in her voice sparked another memory, and this time he grasped it. Peering intently at her, he asked, 'Are you related to old Professor Winthrop? I studied under him. Gavin, I think his name was.'

'He's my father,' she said quietly, picking up her coffee-cup and sipping at the fragrant brew.

'So the old devil is still alive?' he marvelled, wondering if she was older than she looked. Prof Winthrop had been an old white-haired man, long overdue for retirement when he'd studied under him nearly twenty years ago. He vaguely recalled that the professor had had two sons who'd both gone into medicine, but could not recollect any mention of a daughter.

'He must be delighted that someone in the family shares his passion for digging out the little secrets he always claimed were still to be discovered in his field.' He smiled as he spoke, fond memories of the enthusiastic and dedicated old man—and memories of his own youthful drive and ambition!—making him warm towards the pale woman who sat so still across the desk from him.

But, even as he watched, the tentative easiness that he had sensed growing between them disappeared and the faint vestige of colour drained from her face. She became stiff and remote.

'I'm far from finished with the research, but I'll leave the figures I've collated so far with you, if you wish,' she said, deadly polite, but so withdrawn it could have been a different woman. And why should he care?

He nodded and she rose to her feet, obviously deciding that the audience was over.

'I'd be interested in studying it. Maybe we could discuss it again when I've had a look,' he replied, bringing the conversation back to business, as he rose to hold open the door. He would have liked to ask more about her father, to find out if the old man lived locally—if he could perhaps visit him one day. Then he realised something else! He would have liked to keep talking to her. As a colleague, of course.

But she'd shut him out!

He wondered if he'd ever met anyone so prickly, so defensive, so protective of her personal thoughts and feelings that the only time she showed any animation was when she spoke of her work. Could people exist with only their work to fill their lives?

As far as he could discover, Ellen Winthrop could —and possibly did. Maybe he could learn from her. That was what he wanted now, wasn't it?

Then he remembered the phone call she'd made!

CHAPTER THREE

ELLY had always believed that a week which started badly usually improved, but the fates had decided to be less than kind and the days lurched from disaster to disaster with an errant will of their own.

To make matters worse, the new owner, Dr Ballantyne, as she'd discovered his name to be, seemed intent on getting to know every hidden corner of his new domain, and he haunted the corridors like a very large, ominous black shadow, usually bearing down on them at the most inopportune time.

So losing the key was the last straw!

It happened, as crises usually did, at the end of her shift, when she had gone to the desk to find it before checking the drugs with the oncoming sister. As the cry went out it became apparent that the key was missing, and it was Debbie who remembered being at the safe with Jan Williams earlier in the afternoon.

Jan, who'd struggled through most of the day feeling wretched, had finally succumbed to a headache that Elly knew was the onset of the flu strain that beset them. She had sent Jan home, and no doubt the key had gone with her.

'I'm off duty now,' Debbie told her. 'If you give me Jan's address, I'll get a cab out to her place and pick it up.'

'If only it were that easy,' Elly replied, with a wan smile. 'Do you remember when she left?'

'About an hour ago,' was the prompt reply.

'Forty-five minutes, according to the time-sheet.'

Elly pointed to the scrawled signature. 'Do you know what that means?'

She was already dialling a cab, and interrupted her explanation to give Jan's address and instructions to collect the key. If Jan didn't have the key the cab could be cancelled.

'If the key is missing for more than an hour, we have to change the locks!'

She dialled Jan's number now, watching the disbelief in Debbie's face with a wry understanding.

'Health Department regulations, like always having two nurses open the safe, and two nurses present when drugs from it are administered. Losing the key is bad enough but it's nothing to the trouble that ensues when a quantity of drugs goes missing.'

She heard the ringing cease, and Jan's tired voice saying a resentful, 'Hello.'

'It's Ellen Winthrop, Jan—have you got the key?'

The muttered confusion at the end of the phone told her the answer was yes, and she was glad she'd guessed correctly.

'There's a cab on the way to collect it,' she told her. 'It should be there any minute as I rang the cab company first.'

She cut off the apology with soothing assurances. However irritating it might be, she knew no one made these mistakes deliberately. Glancing at the clock, she wondered whether they would make the deadline.

'Why an hour?' Debbie asked, bemused by the urgency and tension she must have been sensing.

'I suppose they needed a cut-off point. It could just as easily have been thirty minutes, although people might drop the key into their pocket and go off to lunch, so the shorter time could be totally disruptive.'

'I meant, why is there a time limit at all? What's the hassle about someone taking the key home? Couldn't there be spare keys?' Debbie sounded quite perplexed by what, to her, must be an example of bureaucracy gone mad!

Elly tried to explain. 'If we have more than one key, it's harder to keep track of the duplicates. There is a spare for each cabinet in the safe in the chief exec's office, but who wants to admit their mistake and go and ask for it?'

'Not me, that's for sure!'

With a smile for the apprehension in the nurse's voice, Elly continued, 'The rules are made for drug security reasons. I know Jan and can understand how the mistake occurred today, but if someone wanted access to the narcotics we keep, the easiest way is to take the key for long enough to make an impression, or get a similar one cut.'

'But that could be done in half an hour, if the person who took the key was organised,' Debbie protested, drawing a slight grin from Elly.

'Of course it could if one knew the right people,' she admitted, 'but rules are rules and I want every minute of this hour if I'm to escape the consequences.'

She patted the young woman on the arm. 'Anyway, it's not your problem. You get off home. You've two days off, haven't you?' she asked, and saw the brightening of the dark eyes and the small smile that accompanied an excited nod.

'Yes, and I'm looking forward to it, although I want to be back on duty when Kathryn returns to the ward.'

Elly nodded. The young girl's recovery had been set back when she had haemorrhaged badly, and had to be returned to Theatre. She would be kept in Intensive Care for a few more days, and all the Neurovascular staff were feeling concerned and unusually pessimistic about the eventual outcome.

'You'll be back,' Elly assured her, 'and your preceptor should also be sufficiently recovered to be back with you. No doubt you'll be pleased about that, as well!' she added with a self-deprecating grin.

She saw the colour sweep into Debbie's cheeks, but the response was unexpected.

'I've learnt more working directly under you than I've learnt since I first started uni,' she said quickly, then turned and hurried off, as if afraid she might have said too much.

Elly watched her go with a feeling of bewilderment. She'd spent more time berating the poor nurse than helping her, she was certain of that, but the hidden compliment pleased her.

Back to business, she reminded herself! Lock changes were an administrative problem, but she would have to report the incident, and was afraid it would not escape the all-seeing eyes of the new owner.

Her relief had turned up and was also watching the clock. Apart from the problem with the locks, Elly could not leave until the drugs had been checked, and a queasy feeling in her stomach reminded her that it was some time since they'd had a discrepancy. If it happened today. . .

'I'm going out to the front door to wait for the cab,' she told the relief, and slipped through the corridors that wound towards the main entrance.

She saw an empty cab pull up and glanced at her watch. Five minutes too late! Then, out of the shade into the sunlight stepped two figures, Debbie in her pale pink nurse graduate uniform, and the dark bulk of Dr Ballantyne. The cab driver had left his seat and was walking round the bonnet, but her eyes were

on the couple, who exchanged warm hugs before
Debbie planted a kiss on the parted lips of the hospital owner then opened the rear door and slid into
the cab.

'You waiting for the key, Miss?' the cabbie was saying, and Elly turned to him with a start, having
forgotten why she was standing at the front door as
she tried to analyse the dismay that had struck her as
she witnessed the little scene.

'Thanks,' she said absentmindedly, signing the chit
the driver presented to her. She remembered seeing
them together in the corridor one morning. Surely
there was nothing in it! Debbie was barely twenty!
That man was not only so much older, but there was
something about him—a bitterness, was it?—that
would spoil all the lovely youthful qualities of the
young woman.

'I am holding this door for you, Sister!'

The words cracked like a whip above her head and
she spun around.

It was in his face, his voice, even his stance, she
reminded herself, as she walked through, passing him
with a vague nod as her mind followed her thoughts.
A kind of world-weary cynicism, as if he had seen and
done everything that life could offer, and found the
experiences wanting. He would soon dull the bright
hope of young Debbie, and tarnish the special shine
of her youth.

'Oh, you've got it, Elly!'

Her relief was hurrying along the passage towards
her, and the words brought her back with a jolt. Why
on earth was she thinking disparaging thoughts about
Dr Ballantyne, a man she barely knew? And as for
Debbie! The young nurse would be off her ward in
another two months, and unlikely to ask if she could

come back when her first year of spending time in different areas was completed.

'It was over the hour!' she said shortly, cutting off any further conversation, while she tried to force her mind to focus on the present and the procedures she would have to put into place to have the locks changed and the relevant authorities notified.

'Let's check the cupboard and I'll do the paperwork for the lock before I leave,' she suggested, when they reached the Neurovascular desk.

Her grim forebodings about the contents of the cupboard were proved false, but it was still dark by the time she left the ward and walked through to Intensive Care to check on Kathryn.

'Far more stable today,' the sister in charge told her, her eyes never leaving the bank of screens that monitored her patients' conditions ceaselessly. 'If there are no more hiccups, you can have her back in a couple of days.'

'No more hiccups?'

'You mustn't have heard! After she came back from surgery the second time, on full blood again, she showed a sharp rise in intracranial pressure. We'd had earlier instructions to use a fifty-gram IV bolus of Mannitol if this happened. It's the most common drug for osmotherapy, and usually prescribed, but we didn't want to give Mannitol conjointly with the blood, because of the pseudoaglutination properties. Of course, as is always the case in an emergency, we couldn't get hold of her surgeon.'

'The second surgical trauma would have increased the oedema as well as the ICP. What did you do?'

'Yelled for help! Dr Ballantyne responded. He suggested the addition of sodium chloride to the Mannitol, as it was an emergency, then he found Kathryn's surgeon and said a few harsh words about not changing instructions after the second visit to Theatre.'

'And she responded to the Mannitol?' Elly hid a shudder at the thought of Dr Ballantyne's 'harsh words'.

'Beautifully, although we are checking urinary output closely, and measuring all fluids in and out. We don't need renal failure, when we've got her safely through this far.'

'Poor kid,' Elly murmured, looking through the glass door where the real person lay, although the screen proof of her existence was more important at this stage.

Walking quietly into the room, she spoke to Mrs Wilson, offering to stay with the sleeping patient while the mother had a break.

'I've just been out,' Mrs Wilson assured her. 'Kathryn's sister took the day off work, and she came in so I could sleep during the day and stay with her tonight.'

'You can't keep it up for too long, you know,' Elly remonstrated quietly.

'Just for another night or two we'll try to be with her,' the woman said firmly. 'It's all the machines and things. We don't want her to wake up and be frightened. She was scared enough going into the operation, without having to put up with this paraphernalia.' She waved her hand around in the air, encompassing the monitors, tubes and wires that kept watch over her daughter's sedated form. Even to Elly, Intensive Care was frighteningly mechanical, taking all the humanity out of patient care, despite saving lives with its expertise.

Elly patted the woman on the arm. 'I do understand, although you'll find she'll remember very little about being in here later on.'

Thinking of Kathryn and the problems that lay ahead of her brought her mind back to Debbie. Was it because she recognised something special in the young woman that she was interested in her future? That little something extra that would make her an excellent nurse?

If she doesn't decide to throw it all in for marriage and kids, Elly mused, wandering absentmindedly towards the car park. She could do both, as Elly had once hoped she might herself, but then, if Debbie married a man rich enough to buy a hospital, there'd be no necessity to work. Careers brought their own personal satisfaction, but most married women she knew worked because they had to, and the fact that they had a satisfying career was simply a bonus.

She was so lost in her thoughts that she didn't notice that the stairway leading down to the car park was dimmer than usual. She pushed through the door and all thinking ceased as the world spun eerily and bright lights flashed behind her eyes. . .

'. . .waiting for the person coming off duty late, and alone,' a deep dark voice was saying. Did voices have colours? she wondered, knowing somehow that they must because she recognised this one as black.

Someone was shining a light in her eyes and she turned her head away from it, thinking of lights that weren't as bright as this. Weren't bright at all! The sudden movement of her head made her wince, and she lifted her hand to try to find the source of the pain, but a large warm hand grasped her arm and held her still and the black voice murmured soothingly.

Black velvet! Wrapping around her shoulders, the soft timbre of the voice stroking against her skin as effectively as the pile of the plush material would.

Now someone was asking questions—stupid

questions about her name and where she lived. She opened her eyes again, and the lights weren't quite as bright. All her senses told her she was in the hospital, so people should know her name. She tried to tell them about the lights not being as bright, but the black voice was talking again, insisting she say her name, not velvety at all now, but rough and hard.

'Ellen Winthrop,' she muttered querulously, 'and I live at Hollywell, but the lights weren't on.'

She felt very tired and her head ached, so she closed her eyes again.

I must be getting the flu, she reasoned, as the persistent, throbbing headache forced her awake a little later. She opened her eyes and a small treatment-room in Gracemere's accident and emergency centre swam into view. A nurse she could not recognise stood at the doorway, looking at her uncertainly.

'Did I fall and hit my head on a step?' Elly asked her, remembering the dim light on what was usually a brightly lit stairway.

'No!' the nurse said hesitantly, adding, 'Can you remember who you are and where you live?' in a timid and quite unprofessional tone.

Elly repeated the required information, and tried to sit up, to reassure the worried nurse that she was OK—apart from a splitting headache.

'Lie back, please,' the woman begged, then ducked out the door.

She was back within minutes, practically bowing the next intruder through into the room. One glance revealed the cause of her anxiety. For some unknown reason, the new hospital owner was personally interested in her health!

'Worried about a compensation claim?' she asked

nastily, her sore head exacerbating the irritation the man's presence always caused.

'Worried that you might have been more badly concussed than you obviously are,' he replied with an acid politeness. 'It seems you're right back to your usual aggressive self!'

'Look who's talking about aggressive,' she muttered, and tried to turn her head away from him, but the pain in her neck put a stop to that defence, so she contented herself with what she hoped was a fulminating glare.

He watched the wince as she tried to move and felt an exasperated concern for this touchy woman who was determined to make sure his takeover of the hospital was as difficult as possible, although it was unlikely she'd intentionally got herself hit on the head to annoy him further!

He thought he'd broken through her deep reserve when they'd spoken about her work, but the defensive wall had been re-erected promptly when he'd crossed some imaginary line with his simple question about her father.

'Do you feel up to answering a few questions?' he asked, hoping his exasperation wasn't revealed in his voice. Somehow, the sight of her lying there, so pale against the vivid red of her hair which had been unbound to allow a thorough examination of her skull, unnerved him. Vulnerable wasn't a word he'd have associated with this fiery dragon, but it kept coming into his mind.

He watched her nod, gingerly, as if assessing each small movement for pain.

'Can you remember coming through the door into the car park?'

She nodded again, her eyes wide with apprehension

as she tried to work out what he was getting at. Wide, and very green. Distractingly green, really. He'd have liked to reach out and pat her, to soothe away the shadow of fear he could see lurking in their depths.

'Do you remember seeing anyone?'

The panic that had been creeping up on Elly flooded forward in a convulsive rush.

'I'm going to be sick,' she muttered, turning desperately away from him, humiliated to be so weak in front of this man who delighted in his power games.

'Here!' He had moved with a speed astonishing in such a big man, round the high bed, to thrust a basin into her hands, and hold her head as she retched repeatedly. When the spasm had passed, he passed her a glass of water, to rinse her mouth, then whisked the basin away, and slid an arm around her shoulders, while he pushed back the mane of hair and wiped her white, frightened face.

'Ted Eames found you unconscious in the car park', he said quietly, stroking her shoulder in a gentle, soothing manner while he said words she found hard to believe. 'Your relief told us you were carrying a handbag when you left the ward, and it is missing.'

He paused, as if to allow her time to assimilate what he was saying. She could have nodded, but it was so very safe and comfortable where she was, her forehead resting against the solid wall of his chest, that she didn't want to move in case he took away the support!

'We've X-rayed your skull, and there's no apparent fracture, but the contusion here——' he ran the fingers of his free hand through her hair to gently rest on the tender portion of her scalp – is consistent with a blow, rather than a fall. That, and the fact that your handbag is missing, seems to point to someone hiding in the car park, someone who hit you from behind as you came through the glass door.'

Now she had to move. She lifted her sore head, and felt him ease his body away from her, although his arm stayed, warm and infinitely comforting, around her shoulders.

'My car? Did they take my car?'

His hand patted her shoulder. 'Your car keys were still in your hand. I'll hold on to them and get one of the orderlies to drive the car to your home for you tomorrow.'

She tried to follow what he was saying, to make some sense of it all!

'Why me?' she asked, then knew it was a stupid question, answering it herself with a quick, 'Because I was running late, and came down alone. At shift changes there are dozens of nurses pouring into the car park.'

'That's what the police think,' he agreed quite casually, although the mention of the word 'police' made her feel sick all over again.

'I must ring home,' she said, her agitation clear in her voice. 'They'll be worrying. Unless the police——' The image the word conjured up was so frightening that she reached out and grasped his arm, shaking it as she looked up into his face. 'The police wouldn't have gone to my house, would they?' she begged, desperately worried by the effect a police car pulling up outside might have on her father.

'I rang your home and spoke to a Mrs Hobson,' he said calmly, as if her hysteria had thrust him back into his role of hospital owner.

Relief washed over her, and then disappointment. She'd liked the brief physical comfort he'd offered, and had welcomed the heaviness of his arm and the solidity of his chest.

'Thank you,' she said faintly, whipping her hand off his arm with an embarrassed jerk. 'They worry!'

She hoped he would take that as an explanation of her panic. It was all he was going to get. Her head was aching with a throbbing persistence that made her long to close her eyes and sleep forever.

'I told the police you weren't fit to be interviewed,' he said, his voice distant, and the formality back in its tone. 'I'll tell them what you've told me, but they will probably still want to speak to you when you're feeling up to it.'

'Thank you,' she mumbled again, knowing it was inadequate but unable to think of an alternative. 'May I go now?'

She swung her legs off the bed, and waited for the swimming sensation the movement caused to go away, before testing her balance.

'Only up to your own ward as a patient—and lie back, you'll be wheeled. You've been concussed and should be under observation for twenty-four hours.'

'But I've got to go,' she told him, adding desperately, 'I'm fine now, and Mrs Hobson is a trained nurse, she can keep an eye on me.'

'She's your housekeeper?' he asked, puzzled by her statement. Who had live-in housekeepers these days? Even his work-shy Jocee had made do with a daily woman and a part-time cook who prepared dinner on the rare evenings they were at home.

Elly nodded painfully. She wasn't up to any further explanations, her thoughts focused now on the old man who might not know who she was, but who did not sleep until she had visited him and said goodnight. He would be soothed by Mrs Hobson's excuses for only so long. After that, his agitation would increase, until it reached a stage where no amount of sedation would blot out his fear, and he would be up, wandering restlessly and repeatedly through a maze of his own making, all night.

'You should stay in,' the man was saying, but without the usual assurance in his voice. 'Will Mrs Hobson know enough to watch for decreasing level of consciousness? Will she check your pupils for abnormal light response? For anisocoria?'

'I'm perfectly all right,' Elly muttered with as much determination as she could muster, trying to remember what anisocoria meant and wondering if she was suffering receptive dysphasia. Maybe she was more concussed than she thought.

'You realise you could have a seizure?' her tormentor persisted. 'Or there could be a basal skull fracture and a CSF leak that we haven't detected.'

'I could have cancer you haven't detected as well,' she replied crossly. 'You are being ridiculous, and I'm too tired to argue.'

Her voice wavered as she spoke, and his opposition crumbled so suddenly that she became suspicious.

Was he worried about the repercussions of this attack, thinking of the possible publicity, the fear and panic that might filter through the staff and adversely affect his smooth-running business. Was he thinking it would be better to have her out of the hospital, so word would not spread like a bushfire?

'I've got to go,' she said stubbornly, and lurched to her feet, grateful for the quick reflexes that shot his arm out to steady her.

There was a muttered curse, and she looked up to see him watching her with a strange expression on his face. She must look a mess, she realised. Her uniform in disarray, her hair waving in wild confusion about her face.

She was so close that he could feel the warmth of her body, and smell a faint femaleness on her skin. He should have insisted on her staying, he knew that, but she'd become so agitated when he'd suggested it that it had been impossible to argue.

Now here she was, tottering on her feet, her head flung up in challenge as her eyes dared him to stop her. His glance shied away from the valiant defiance in those mysterious green depths, slid down the slim pale neck, over skin so fine he could see the blue of veins and white of tendons through it. Her crisp white uniform was rumpled, a button torn off the front, so that it gaped, revealing the soft rise of milk-white breasts, and a dusting of golden freckles in the deep shadow between them.

A surge of blind fury at the unknown assailant who had injured her shot through him, followed by a stirring of something that wasn't pity, and made him feel deeply ashamed.

'I'll drive you home,' he said brusquely, although he wanted to walk away from her, to escape some aura of femininity she had suddenly acquired with her helplessness.

She wouldn't thank you for that sexist thought, he reminded himself grimly, guiding her shaky footsteps out into the brightly lit corridor that ran through the treatment-rooms at the accident and emergency centre.

Get her safely home, that was all he had to do, then forget she was anything other than the strong-willed, efficient machine that ran Neurovascular like a well-drilled army unit.

'I can walk by myself,' she muttered at him, and he recognised the warmth of embarrassment creeping through the skin beneath his hand. Did the stupid woman think people would read anything into his helping her out to the car?

'If I let go of you, you'll fall,' he muttered back, smiling at the interested onlookers who poked their heads up from desks, and out of treatment-rooms. 'I'm taking Sister Winthrop home,' he told the night receptionist. 'Phone through to Neurovascular and let them know she's not going up there. Assure the sister in charge that I'll see she's all right before I leave her. She was very concerned.'

Elly sank into the soft leather seat of the man's car with a sense of vast relief. Closing her eyes, she eased her head cautiously back on to the rest, finding a spot that was comfortable, and breathed deeply. Maybe she should have stayed in the ward overnight, she decided, as waves of nausea washed over her. Better than throwing up in the boss's car, she told herself, then was pleased to realise her sense of humour still worked— warped though it might be!

The driver's door opened and he slid in beside her, impossibly large in the close confines of the car, a whiff of sharply scented aftershave mingling with the leathery interior to underline his maleness.

'I checked your address,' he said, and she opened her eyes to peer across at him, seeing the straight profile against the light outside the car. 'It's down near the Runaway Bay Marina, isn't it?'

She nodded, and he reached out and touched her shoulder.

'I'll get that far and you can tell me where to go after that. Are you sure you feel up to this?'

His voice wrapped around her again, offering comfort and security. For a brief moment she longed to snuggle down in the seat and give herself up to his tender concern—to let someone else do the worrying!

'I must do my hair,' she said as she nodded her confirmation. Maybe she could banish these unlikely fancies with practical matters. 'Would you have a comb?'

For the first time the theft of her handbag became a reality, and she wondered vaguely what else beside a comb she would have had in it.

'Leave your hair,' he ordered as he fired the engine. 'Combing it will hurt your head. Besides, it's nice hair and doesn't deserve to spend all its time bound up in such a monstrously tight braid.'

'It fluffs out all over the place if I don't do it tightly,' she explained, while part of her mind wondered if this was a rational conversation or the demented ravings of concussion. 'But I do need a comb. I need to tidy it up, pull it back at least, before I get home.'

'Afraid whoever is waiting for you will think you've been having a wild night?' her chauffeur said nastily and she decided she must still be concussed. This was definitely not a normal conversation.

'I need to do my hair,' she repeated stubbornly, feeling stupid tears smarting in her eyes because he was making things difficult for her.

'There's a comb in the glove-box,' he said coldly. There was probably an entire make-up kit in there if the stupid woman needed it. She was so impossibly pale that she looked like a freakish, red-headed ghost, yet she was worried whoever awaited her at home would be concerned if her hair was untidy.

The trouble with women was that they could never get their priorities right, he decided angrily, watching her shudder with the pain as she dragged the comb through her hair.

'Is it right here?' he asked as they passed cluster of

shops and forest of tall masts at the Marina.

As she murmured her assent he swung the car off
the main road, and was startled by the silvery moonlit
waters shimmering at the end of the street.

'Left at the end,' she said in a muffled voice, scrab-
bling in the glove box for some other beauty aid, while
he gazed in awe at the magnificence of the stretch of
water the locals accepted so casually.

'It's number seven, up the other end,' she directed,
twisting the hair that had fascinated him into a knot
at the back of her head, her lips tightly compressed as
she forced her arms to obey her mind's instructions,
when all she must want to do was lie down and sleep.

The front of the house was unprepossessing—flat,
old-fashioned, haphazardly put together, as if bits were
added at the whim of the occupants rather than with
any eye for style or outward beauty. The upper storey
was in darkness, but he could see the windows that
stretched along the front to grab every centimetre of
the fabulous outlook. Downstairs, a dim light burned
in the front room, which was curtained in a hazy gauze-
like material. Whoever was in there could probably
see out, while retaining their own privacy, he decided,
as he walked swiftly round the car to help his stubborn
passenger struggle to her feet.

The front door opened as he steadied her, and a
small, plump, anxious-looking woman peered out, then
hurried forward when she saw the person who was
trying to pull away from his supporting hand.

'You should have stayed in the hospital, Elly,' she
clucked, hovering around their slow progress like an
anxious mother hen. 'One sleepless night doesn't hurt
Hobson or me. I've told you that again and again!'
she scolded. 'And if you're a doctor, you should have
seen she stayed there,' she added, glaring at Gregor.

'Have you ever been able to tell this woman what to do?' he asked, and through the pain and confusion Elly thought she heard a note of laughter in his voice.

'Thank you for bringing me home,' she said, with the formal politeness of a child reciting learnt words. 'I'll be fine now.'

'Trying to get rid of me, Sister?' he asked as they reached the open door, and he had a glimpse of a small ante-room leading off to the left, and some stairs ahead, that must give access to the upper part of the house. He had an immediate impression of colour, and greenery. There was something warm and welcoming about the glimpse, something homey and comfortable that he did not associate with the ice-cool image of Sister Winthrop.

Elly! He tasted the word on his tongue, and found he liked it. Then the strained anxiety in her voice brought him sharply back to reality.

'Please, please go!' she was pleading, and he could feel the tension in the trembling limb he held so firmly.

She did not want him in that inviting sanctuary— the message was coming through loud and clear. He handed her over to Mrs Hobson, and turned away, furious with her for her tenacious rejection of further help and puzzled by his own reactions to her intransigence.

'See she goes straight to bed, and make sure she's not back at the hospital for at least a week,' he ordered abruptly, handing his patient over to Mrs Hobson and trying to hide the anger in a frosty politeness. 'And get her own doctor to look at her tomorrow. If there's any sign of continued headaches, dizziness or nausea, get her back up to Accident and Emergency.'

'I'll take good care of her, sir,' the older woman said, but her placatory words only exacerbated his distress.

'I can't think why I agreed to let her come home in the first place,' he fumed.

'She probably insisted,' Mrs Hobson said with an understanding smile. 'Goodnight, sir,' she added, propelling his injured employee through the door and closing it firmly behind them both

CHAPTER FOUR

'THAT'S your boss on the phone again,' Mrs Hobson called up the stairs. 'Wants to know if you're up to a visit from the police. Do you want to speak to him?'

Elly looked at the phone by the bed, then out through the glassed-in veranda to the dancing water beyond.

Of course she didn't *want* to speak to him, but he had rung several times, to enquire about her recovery, and now there were a few things she should get straightened out.

'I'll take it, Mrs Hobson,' she called and picked up the receiver with slow, cold fingers.

'How are you feeling?' he barked, none of the sympathy she half expected to hear in his deep voice.

'I'm better,' she said firmly. Well, compared to yesterday, through which she'd dozed and slept and couldn't remember at all, she was!

'The police want a statement,' he went on. 'Are you up to it?'

'I'm better,' she repeated fussily. 'I can see them any time it suits them. Who should I call to make the arrangements?'

'I'll make the arrangements,' he argued. 'I'll tell them eleven o'clock, then you can have an undisturbed sleep after your lunch.'

She was distracted by his firmness. There was something so fussily pedantic about the way he spoke that she was reminded of her father, back when he had spoilt and cosseted her when she was ill—back when he knew who she was!

'I wanted to speak to you,' she said quickly, thrusting away memories that threatened to overcome her. 'I rang the ward and they said that you said I wouldn't be back for a week. I'm better,' she insisted, then cringed at the repetitiveness that made her sound half-witted. 'I'm rostered off-duty today and tomorrow anyway, but I'll be back at work on Friday. I've already let the roster clerk know.'

'And I've told her you won't be back till Monday. I'll see you at eleven!'

There was a sharp click as he hung up, and she was left staring at the phone, her stomach clenching as she absorbed what he had said.

'Mrs Hobson!' she yelled, then stood up far too suddenly causing a sharp pain to stab through her head. She slumped back against the pillows, pulling the quilt up around her shoulders as if suddenly chilled to the bone.

'Hobson and I will take your father for a walk along the front,' the housekeeper assured her when she explained about the police. 'It's such a lovely day we were going to have morning tea across the road. We'll just go a little further along, so he won't notice the police car at the house.'

Elly nodded, and wondered why she was still shaking. She should be relieved that the illustrious Dr Ballantyne was concerned enough to want to be here when the police came. He was probably still thinking of his own liability.

That was why he had sounded so annoyed on the phone. All this fuss over one nurse's broken head must be distracting him from his timetable of zealous reform.

'I've baked a tea-cake and peanut biscuits. I'll bring

some up for you to have with coffee when the policeman comes,' Mrs Hobson was saying, fluttering along
the veranda fluffing up cushions she'd already shaken
when she'd swept and dusted earlier in the morning.

'I'm sure policemen don't need coffee and cakes,'
Elly objected, thinking that it was a little intimacy she
didn't want to share with Dr Ballantyne.

'All gentlemen like coffee and cakes,' Mrs Hobson
told her with an emphatic nod of her neat grey head.
'I'll set it on the table out here. In fact, I'll go up with
Hobson to settle your father, then come back and fix
the coffee for you.'

'I'm not an invalid,' Elly protested. 'I can easily
make a pot of coffee. So, for that matter, could Dr
Ballantyne, seeing he's insisting on being present at
this interview.'

'I'll do it,' was all Mrs Hobson replied, disappearing
towards the stairs before Elly could think of another
objection.

'People keep bossing me around, Fran,' she told the
cat that was curled comfortably on the foot of her bed.
Blue eyes regarded her steadily for a moment, then
Franny blinked, as if surprised by the statement, and
stretched her limbs in a show of total unconcern for
her mistress's predicament.

With slow reluctance, Elly eased out of the bed.
She'd have to shower and dress. Not only dress, but
put on something that would give her some colour, to
press home her claim of being 'better'!

The sun might be shining brightly, but the old house
still had a wintry chill about it. They could sit on the
veranda; it was warm and sunny out there.

She settled on red stirrup pants and a light, knitted
silk sweater in a tawny mix of orange and pink. It had
been a daring buy with her colouring, but had suited

her so well that it had become a favourite. Smoothing cream into her face, she sighed at the paleness, and cheated with a light touch of cream blusher under a fine coating of powder.

With swift assurance she brushed mascara on to her golden lashes, and darkened her pale brows, then finished her preparations with a special lipstick she had found which matched the sweater exactly. Surveying the result, she could not repress a feeling of satisfaction. She wasn't all that bad-looking! she assured herself, out of the ghastly white of the ward sister uniform, and with a little bit of warpaint in place.

Then she wondered why the assurance was so necessary. The policeman wouldn't care what she looked like, and Dr Ballantyne had seen her at her worst.

You need to look well and healthy, she reminded herself dragging her mind away from the memory. She turned from the mirror to watch the little procession cross the front yard and amble along the street. Her father, slumped in the wheelchair they used to make the walk along the road more pleasurable for everyone, his head turning anxiously this way and that, although he had walked this street for sixty years.

Mr Hobson pushed the chair. Small, thin and wiry, but immensely strong, he was able to support her father's weight, and lift him when his legs grew unsteady. Mrs Hobson, looking like a mobile mushroom under her huge hat, trotted along behind, the picnic basket over one arm while she waved the other in greeting to the neighbours.

It was a friendly street, Elly admitted to herself, as she heard the echo of the calls, and knew that someone would cross the road and sit with the little group at the far picnic table, talking naturally, as if her father's condition did not exist, including him in the genial chit-chat that eased the pressures of the day.

Then the unfamiliar car turned the corner, slowing as it passed the pedestrians, then speeding up again to swing into her drive. Dark green, a Lexus, she realised now.

'It must be the dreaded Dr B.,' she told the cat, who had moved to her favourite spot on the front window-ledge and was watching the scene with a bored indifference. 'He's early.'

Reluctance to face him again glued her feet to the floor. She stared out of the window, seeing Mrs Hobson pass the picnic basket to her husband, and turn to hurry back towards the house as the big car came to a quiet halt.

The driver's door opened silently, and the man unfurled himself from behind the wheel, turning towards the sheet of water and staring out across the blue and green and aquamarine brilliance to the low tree-clad sand dunes of South Stradbroke Island.

She saw his shoulders, bulky from behind, under the well-cut jacket, lift and drop. It was as if he had drawn a deep breath. Rejuvenating his soul with the beauty of the scene, or simply sighing with frustration at the trouble she was causing?

How could anyone who awoke to such beauty be as cantankerous as his Sister Winthrop, Gregor wondered, tasting the salt in the light breeze off the water, and watching two skiffs catch it in their sails and skim past. It was years since he'd sailed! Years since he'd done anything but work, really.

He breathed deeply, dragging the air deep into his lungs as if he could somehow imbibe the fresh clarity of the day and make it part of him.

'Good morning!' The housekeeper's salute brought him back to reality, and he turned towards the stout figure who hurried down the street towards him.

He hadn't recognised her under the big hat, but now realised she'd been with the old man who was being wheeled along the road, up near the corner.

He peered in that direction, as an unwelcome suspicion crossed his mind. The elderly man in the chair! He'd felt a flash of recognition, then, unable to pin it down, had dismissed it. Had it been his old professor? And, if so, was this woman so unable to come to terms with whatever illness he suffered, that she'd sent her own father from the house to avoid having a past student meet up with him again.

'Elly's flat is upstairs,' Mrs Hobson was saying, hovering patiently by the door while he chased the threads of his thoughts.

Two nights ago he had wanted to walk through this door, to see if the world someone had created behind it was as comfortable and inviting as one brief glimpse had suggested. Now, he was filled with a curious reluctance, as if the place might be poisoned by his thoughts —or by the action of the woman who was waiting for him upstairs.

'Here's the police now,' Mrs Hobson said, looking beyond him to the marked car that had come round the other corner and stopped at the kerb.

It was an excuse to wait!

Elly shifted from one foot to another, uncertain whether she should walk downstairs and greet the uninvited guests, or remain where she was and let Mrs Hobson play butler.

She felt safer up here, she decided, then wondered what possible danger there was from which to feel 'safer'. At least if she stayed up here she didn't have to bring the inquisitive man past her father's flat and explain or answer questions about its use.

She waited.

The entrance was as warm and welcoming as he'd imagined. There was a vague Mediterranean flavour about the furnishing, although it was uniquely Australian. Maybe it was the terracotta colour in the painted concrete floor, and the creamy pink of the walls. The healthy blackboy plant with its tall spike of flower, and the lush tree-fern that nestled in another corner, were certainly indigenous, and went well with the Aboriginal painting that hung on the one unbroken wall.

Off to the left was a small room with a practical hat-stand festooned with hats, and a large carved chest. Beyond this entrance, he glimpsed a sitting-room that echoed the feeling of relaxation, warmth and welcome. Yet the very ambience of the place unsettled him! It was definitely at odds with the cold, efficient woman he knew of from the hospital, and with a person who would summarily dismiss her own father from the house when guests arrived.

Mrs Hobson greeted the policeman then led them up narrow stairs that turned at right angles to lead arriving guests into an open room that obviously combined the function of sitting- and dining-room. It was a strange mixture of colours and styles, rich, yet not obtrusive, but his eyes did not take in the details, drawn as they were to the glassed-in veranda and the beauty of the view beyond the windows.

'Good morning, I'm Ellen Winthrop.'

She must have come from behind them, and he turned to see her shaking hands with the policeman, murmuring something he could not hear as her slim white hand rested in the man's large, meaty one.

It definitely was her, his numb brain insisted, but he found the change from the white authoritarian to this slim vibrant being too much to absorb all at once.

'Dr Ballantyne!' She inclined her head with the grace of a royal relative bestowing a kindly acknowledgement on a less exalted mortal.

'It's warmer and more comfortable on the veranda,' she was saying, as he puzzled over the change in the woman, and his own reaction to it.

She led the way, waving a languid hand towards the cane chairs with worn fat cushions that spoke of use and comfort.

He hurried forward, hoping to get the one that was closer to the chair she obviously used, an open book face down on the little table beside it. It was only because he wanted to get a closer look at her face, he told himself, subsiding half resentfully into the further chair as the policeman beat him with a smart manoeuvre. This was obviously some act she was putting on, and the brave colours and painted face were an attempt to show him she was well enough to return to the hospital.

'It won't work, you know,' he said abruptly, the words coming out more loudly than he'd intended.

The policeman turned to him with a cocked eyebrow, but he ignored the unspoken question and added pointedly, 'You are not to return to work until Monday.'

The policeman lost interest in him then, opening his notebook and turning to Sister Winthrop with an eagerness Gregor found distasteful. Mrs Hobson bustled in with a low table that she set up equidistant from the three of them, then returned with plates of cake and biscuits, mugs, milk and sugar, then finally a pot of coffee, its aroma wafting round the room, adding to the enticement of its homeliness.

I must shift out of the hotel, he decided, ignoring the murmur of question and answer. Find myself a flat. He looked around, suddenly intrigued by his surroundings. Beyond where they sat, another room opened on to this veranda, and he could see enough to imagine it was a bedroom. See enough to make him want to see more!

Ellen was offering the policeman coffee, leaning forward to pour it. She looked up at him, an unspoken question in her bright eyes, and he nodded, then stood up, using the excuse of picking up the coffee to move further down the veranda. This is ridiculous, he told himself, but he had seen the cat now, and knew it would be acceptable—just—to walk across and scratch between its ears.

The french doors opened wide enough to give the impression that the room had only three walls, and the big brass bed was positioned so that the last thing she saw at night and the first thing she saw each morning would be the water.

She—or they?

He looked again, and shook his head in a definite denial.

It was a woman's room! Serenely beautiful in white, with snatches of green in every shade from the palest lime to the deepest emerald. Cushions, ribbons, hat bands, plants and curtain bindings all had their contribution to make. Distinctively feminine, with no hint of male occupation; distinctively *this* woman's room! Then the fact that he saw her as a woman, not a colleague or a member of his staff, hit him with a startling intensity.

'I am sorry I can't be more help,' she was saying behind him, as he tickled the cat beneath the chin and tried to restore order to his thoughts. 'I wrote a list of what was in my handbag,' she added, standing up and turning towards where he stood. 'I'll get it.'

She crossed to the bedroom, ignoring him completely as she went straight to a small desk that stood against the far wall. She took a bright splash of colour into the room, and, for a moment he thought he had grasped some secret knowledge of the woman, but the essence of the tiny spark of insight eluded him.

Now she was back, and the policeman was preparing to leave. He wasn't sure what to do next, and the uncertainty fazed him. Prevarication was not in his nature. He should leave, of course! He'd come to support her through the ordeal of the police interview, but the vulnerability he had imagined was gone, and, in its place, was not the calm assurance of his efficient ward sister, but a relaxed, mature, exceedingly—disturbingly?—attractive woman.

He followed the policeman towards the stairs, unable to think of a single reason to prolong his visit, although he would have liked to stay on that sunny veranda for a lot longer.

'Do you use the water much?' he asked, unable to simply walk away after the policeman had driven off.

'I used to,' she said, 'but recently. . .'

The slim shoulders lifted in a shrug, and he imagined he saw a shadow pass across her face.

'Sailing?' he persisted, and saw the bright head nod.

'And swimming, fishing, paddling, and windsurfing,' she added, with a smile that told him how much she had enjoyed it all. 'The back yard is full of gear, but it's only used when one or other of my brothers is up for a holiday with their kids.'

I used to sail and fish and wind-surf, he wanted to say, but he was afraid of her response—or was he more afraid of his own disappointment if it did not meet his expectations? Jocee had professed to love water sports when they were courting, but, once married, she had refused to join him, insisting that the wind and water dried out her skin or tangled her hair.

He looked at the woman standing so silently beside him and an image of her wild red hair flying behind her as she shot across the water on a windsurfer, etched itself in his subconscious mind.

'I'd like the doctor in A and E to check you out before you come back to work on Monday,' was all he said, while he wondered if it might be premature senility, this habit of seeing visions of this woman so clearly in his mind.

Elly bit her tongue, refusing to argue without medical evidence to back up her claim that she was well again. She nodded agreement, and watched him walk across to his car and drive away.

'Seems a nice man,' Mrs Hobson remarked as she walked out to the footpath and turned to rejoin her husband up the road.

'Nice enough to hold the basin while I threw up,' Elly said, a soft smile twisting her lips as the hazy recollection surfaced in her still-jumbled brain.

'If he's a doctor, he wouldn't mind something like that.' Mrs Hobson threw the words back over her shoulder, and Elly wondered what she was suggesting.

Back inside, she rang the hospital and, after answering solicitous enquiries about her health, was put through to what she considered to be 'her' ward.

'Kathryn Wilson came back to us today,' the relief sister told her, with a note of genuine concern in her voice.

'So?' Elly asked, hoping that the woman would spell out her worries.

'She's been heavily sedated, but we have to start cutting back on that. With the wadding and bandages she's deaf at present, whether that's the eventual outcome or not, and when she does wake up she becomes startled and extremely fearful.'

'That's natural enough,' Elly assured her, 'but you can't keep her sedated forever.'

'I know,' was the quick response. 'Intensive Care was concerned enough to warn us about this. She's OK when one of the family is with her during the day, but last night her mother didn't stay and Kathryn woke and panicked. She tangled all the drips and tubes before anyone could get into the room.'

'Can the family afford to pay a "special" for her,' Elly asked, knowing that the hospital staffing would not allow for a nurse to be beside one patient all night every night until she settled down.

'They're battling to pay the fees as it is,' was the doleful reply. 'The night staff will just have to do the best they can.'

'What time does the last member of the family leave?' Elly asked, her mind already considering an idea that might relieve her own boredom until the tyrant allowed her to return to work.

'Her sister has to leave by ten o'clock. She works during the day and comes straight from the office. Her mother has been going home when she arrives and, usually comes back at about six in the morning. They were there around the clock for the first few nights in Intensive Care, but they can't keep it up indefinitely, especially as the mother will still have a big nursing task when Kathryn goes home.'

No one need know, Elly reasoned, and it's better than sitting around at home.

She said quietly, 'I'm feeling fine, and could easily sit with her at night. Tell the night sister I'll come in at ten, but don't make a fuss about it. I'd just as soon it didn't reach the new boss's ears; he's been waving his authoritarian stick over me ever since I was concussed.'

'Been hitting a woman when she's down, has he?'

Elly chuckled at the sympathetic humour in the words. 'Taking advantage of a passing weakness, that's all!' she warned. 'I'll have to be on my toes to see he doesn't exploit it! I've got my tyrannical reputation to protect. What doctor is going to remain properly subservient to my wishes in the ward if he hears a mere hospital owner has got the better of me?'

Her friend laughed now as well. 'You've certainly got them all bluffed,' she agreed, 'but the man might have a point. Are you well enough to come in tonight?'

'Concussed footballers go back on the field after half-time!' Elly reminded her. 'It isn't as if I'll have to do anything. I won't even have to use my concussed brain—just sit and be there if she wakes. I'll manage that!'

'It would be great. I know the night staff will be most relieved.'

It was a long time since she'd done any night-duty, Elly realised, as she sat in a chair by Kathryn's bed, and listened to the almost inaudible hum of the hospital. It was an alien atmosphere, without the bustle and noise, the ringing phone, screeching trolleys and calling voices of the day shifts.

She had turned on a night light, and seated herself where Kathryn could see her if she opened her eyes. The whiteboard and pen she had used the day Kathryn was admitted were on her knee, with the message, 'Hi, I'm Elly Winthrop and I met you on the day you came in,' already printed on it.

She read through Kathryn's file as she waited, but there was little on it about the operation, and she had no idea of the surgeon's prognosis. Looking at the unbandaged part of the pale face with its halo of fine, fair hair, she found herself hoping desperately that some hearing had been saved.

'And just what do you think you are doing here?' The sibilant whisper seemed to pierce the skin at the back of her neck and she slid down further into the chair, not wanting to turn and face the man she knew must be standing right behind her.

'I'm well enough to be sitting with Kathryn for a few hours!' she muttered, disconcerted to find that he'd lifted the second chair from against the wall and placed it right up against hers.

'Intensive Care wouldn't have released her if they thought she still needed twenty-four-hour monitoring,' he snapped, as he dropped down to her level and turned his head towards her, bringing his face so close she could see the dark shadow of his beard beneath his smooth tanned skin. 'The night staff can do two-hourly checks; surely that's sufficient.'

'From a medical point of view, it's more than sufficient,' she said, her eyes turning away from the distraction of beard shadows, back to the sleeping figure on the bed. 'But in nursing we have to consider any number of non-medical factors that will affect the patient's recovery.'

'That sounds like a line straight out of a text-book, Sister Winthrop. Perhaps you can enlighten a poor "medical" person?'

She glanced quickly at him to see if he was joking, but his lips were set in a grim line, and his jaw had a determination about it that told her he wasn't going to like any explanation she might provide.

'Kathryn has been heavily sedated. Intensive Care started cutting back on the dosage and last night she woke and became totally disorientated. She had pulled out her drips before anyone could get to her. Although she's been given sedation for the night, with the reduction of the other drugs the staff aren't certain that she'll sleep through the night.'

'So you're aiming to sit here all night just in case she wakes up, to save the staff the hassle of doing extra checks.'

He sounded furious! Although whispered, the words held a menace that stabbed through her body. Yet she had to fight him, had to stand up to his attempted domination, because she suddenly knew that, if she did give in, she would be changed—weakened—somehow.

'It's nothing to do with the staff,' she hissed, swallowing the 'you big stupid oaf' appellation that had sprung to her lips again. 'It's to do with Kathryn and her well-being, and eventual recovery. She's disorientated enough being unable to hear, without waking in a dark strange room without a friendly face anywhere in sight.'

She kept her eyes on the motionless patient as she spoke, so could not gauge his reaction, but as he did not speak, she continued. 'At least, if I'm here, she has someone to reach out and touch. Her isolation will be bad enough in the future, if she has lost her hearing in that ear, without us condemning her to it now!'

This statement was greeted by a stony silence, but she refused to break it.

'Do you really believe there are no ends, but only new beginnings?' he asked at last, the menace gone from his voice, replaced by something that sounded almost like doubt.

The sudden shift in the conversation threw Elly for a moment and she spun around to face him, wondering where he'd heard words she knew she had said but not to him. He was regarding her intently, his dark grey eyes unreadable in the shaded light, but a stillness in his face that suggested her answer might matter to him.

'How do you know I said that?' she asked, delaying a reply that might reveal too much of herself to this man. For some reason she believed such a revelation would weaken her, make her vulnerable to him in some strange way.

'Debbie told me you said it when she was upset over the potential deafness of this patient.'

Debbie told him! The name had an unsettling familiarity on his tongue. The scene outside the hospital flashed into her mind, making her feel queasy and ill-at-ease. She turned back to watch the sleeping girl, who could not hear their conversation and, quite possibly, would never hear again.

'I do believe it,' she said slowly, testing each word as she tried to ignore the disquiet his use of Debbie's name had caused. 'If one part of your life seems to finish, if a direction you have taken comes to a dead end, surely it's better to go on to the next part instead of wasting effort trying to force yourself further along a track that isn't there, or wasting time on regrets for what might have been.'

'Easier said than done, surely?'

The cynicism of his statement cut through her straying thoughts.

'Everything's easier said than done,' she told him waspishly, taking her eyes off Kathryn for long enough to glare at him. 'I didn't say it would be easy for her, but if she is deaf after this operation, there will be things she can do to overcome the disability, new challenges in learning how to operate in a silent world, and how to compensate for her loss with her other senses. Surely it's better to see it as a new beginning than as an end?'

'Quite the philosopher, aren't you? he murmured, and she sought but did not find the sarcasm she'd expected to hear.

Glancing sideways at him, she saw his head was bent, then, as she was about to look away, she caught a movement, and watched surreptitiously as he pulled his hands out of his pockets and rested them on his knees. Shock and pity washed across her, yet, even as she glimpsed the distorted knuckles she knew she did not want him to know that she had seen.

Without moving her head, she let her eyes turn back to rest on Kathryn, still peacefully asleep. Had the arthritis that was so visible interfered with his work? Had he bought into the hospital for practical as opposed to mercenary reasons? Had the loss of movement in his fingers, the periodic pain of the swollen joints, brought his planned highway through life to an abrupt end?

'Do you always wander round the hospital this late at night?' she asked, when the silence became unbearable and her neck grew stiff from the effort of not looking back at his hands.

'Very rarely,' he admitted. 'I'd been out to dinner and was driving back to my hotel when I began to wonder about something I'd heard about an acoustic neuroma patient who was already deaf in one ear from an earlier accident.'

He paused for so long that Elly wondered if that was all he was going to say, then she felt, rather than saw him shrug, and sensed that he had tucked his hands back into his pockets, but whether to hide them from her eyes or his own, she could not guess.

'I wanted to read the file, to see if there might be a possibility. . .'

The strong deep voice trailed away, and the silence descended again.

'I was a neurosurgeon,' he said at last, and, sensitive in the hushed atmosphere to the nuances in his speech, she detected a deep, harsh anger behind the circumspect delivery. 'Especially interested in the structure and function of nerves. I went into microsurgery, smaller and smaller, looking always to see how far we could go with the tiny threads that can give meaning and depth to our lives by providing our awareness of the world around us.'

On the bed, Kathryn stirred, and Elly rose, then slipped back down into her chair when she realised her charge was not going to wake.

'Were you thinking of the possibility of transplanting the nerve from her deaf ear? Was that what you wanted to check on her file?'

Her amazement at such a concept must have been obvious in her voice, for he replied drily, 'If it happened that her original deafness was caused by inner ear not nerve damage, then the nerve might be usable and I might have suggested possibilities to her surgeon, but I was thinking of doing precisely nothing, Sister Winthrop. For all your Pollyanna-isms, I know that I'm at the end of my chosen road, and I find I have little enthusiasm for new beginnings that aren't of my own choosing.'

The tiny spring of hope was replaced by a vast, depressing sense of defeat, and as Kathryn moved restlessly again, Elly stood up, to be by the bed and in full view if she awoke.

'At least you've had a recognisable end to one part of your life; there are worse scenarios!' she told him with a bitterness that sprang from her own feeling of stagnation in a situation beyond her control.

CHAPTER FIVE

As KATHRYN's eyes flew open and she jerked up in panic, Elly held up the whiteboard with one hand and smiled reassuringly. Her free hand reached out to clasp Kathryn's, to squeeze and massage the fingers that were clenched in fear.

Propping the board against the bed, she rubbed out the first message and wrote, 'Can I get you something?'

'My back's sore,' Kathryn whispered hoarsely.

'I'll rub it if you roll over very carefully on to your good side. Would you like a drink first?' Elly scribbled.

This time, as she turned the board back to her patient, she said the words aloud, so Kathryn, if she looked, would see the lip movements. She mimed drinking from a glass and saw the young woman nod, then added another message, 'I'll be right back,' and smiled reassuringly down at her apprehensive patient.

As she turned to go, she realised that her companion was still sitting in the room, watching her antics with sardonic glee. Determined to ignore him, she flounced away, returning with a glass of fresh orange juice and some sweet-smelling analgesic cream.

Kathryn was still on her back, the whiteboard in her hands. As Elly drew closer, she turned it shyly around and showed Elly what she had written, pointing to the intruder at the same time.

'Is that your boyfriend?' Elly read, and felt embarrassment burn into her skin.

'No!' she said firmly, shaking her head to emphasize the denial. She could only hope he hadn't seen it, she

79

thought, as she passed Kathryn the juice and scrubbed the offending words off the board with a clean tissue from the box by Kathryn's bed.

After setting down the empty glass, she helped her patient roll on to her unbandaged side, then, covering her to the waist with the sheet, she began to rub her back with long, soothing strokes.

'I can see why you're a good nurse. You get everything done, but you don't fuss or bustle.'

The deep voice startled her, as she'd almost forgotten his presence in the room. Almost!

Her body had developed a sensory awareness of this man. Because he was the new owner of the hospital and she was alert to his presence within his domain, or because he was a man?

The 'or' didn't bear thinking about, she told herself, as she eased the strokes to a gentle smoothing as she sensed Kathryn sinking back to sleep. It was a long time since she had even considered that a man might have a place in her personal life. And to think of this man in those terms was nothing short of ridiculous.

He had looks and power and money—a combination that would attract beautiful women as nectar attracted bees. Scrawny red-headed ward sisters wouldn't be high on his list of desirable partners.

She drew the covers up over Kathryn's shoulders, and stepped back away from the bed, then turned to pick up her chair and move it to the other side of the room, so she would again be in Kathryn's line of sight if she awoke.

'I'll shift the chair for you,' he said, and she wondered if she'd imagined the earlier compliment when she heard the grating harshness back in his voice. 'I suppose this is your way of defying my orders,' he added, after watching her sit down with the board and pen by her side.

'It's my way of doing something to help someone else,' she replied with a careful lack of emphasis. 'If I were at home, I'd be sleeping at night and sitting around all day. I'm doing the same thing in here, only the other way around.'

'Did you drive in?' he barked, and she realised she'd annoyed him even more with her sweet reasonableness.

'No,' she admitted, remembering how the idea of driving into the dark car park had made her shiver with an unfamiliar terror, but she could hardly tell him that. She smiled up at him, hoping to cover the shame her weakness had provoked. 'I came by cab.'

For a moment she believed he was going to smile back, and she found herself holding her breath as she waited for the softening effect she imagined it would have on his set face. Then the instant passed, and a frown gathered between the black brows.

'See that the hospital reimburses you,' he said. 'I have a man patrolling the car park at night, but I'd prefer you to take a taxi for the first few weeks back at work.'

He practically threw the words at her, then spun around with surprising speed for such a large man, and disappeared through the door.

Why did she affect him the way she did? he wondered as he stalked back through the practically deserted corridors towards the car park stairs. Coming into that dimly lit room, and seeing the long length of her, the black jeans and sweater a perfect foil for the brightness of her hair, had not only startled him, but filled him with a strange sensation he could not analyse.

Surely, it was simply anger at her intransigent attitude!

Yet the thought of her going back into the car park filled him with an unease that was closer to horror than concern. Damn the woman! It was as if she'd set herself to annoy and aggravate, to cause him trouble ever since he'd arrived at the hospital! Before that, really, because the more he'd heard about the dragon who ran Neurovascular—the ward he was most interested in—the unhappier he'd been.

He knew now that she was a top-notch sister, and the difficult ward ran like a dream, but. . . His mind returned to the tall figure stretched out in the chair, her pale skin stretched across the neat features, and her hair held primly back from her face by two ebony combs.

She had looked tremendously attractive in the bright colours of this morning, and the dull matt finish of the black sweater she wore tonight had given a delicate translucence to her skin; but he pictured her also in a deep rich cream colour—with heavy lace edging draped tantalising across her——

The image was obliterated with an almost physical effort. He was doing it again! Had the woman decked out in a négligé this time!

Keeping watch over her sleeping patient, Elly turned the strange little episode over in her mind. It had been less a conversation than a collection of random statements, with a few transitory glimpses of the man behind the persona of the new hospital owner, tantalising hints at a character that was both complex and, she suspected, somewhat tortured.

She tried to think herself inside his skin, to imagine the desperation and despair he must have known as

his career became less and less possible with the devel-
opment of his disease. Would it have turned her bitter,
made her turn her back completely on the practice of
medicine, on the research that might bring hope to so
many people's futures?

You've put your own career on hold, an inner voice
argued, but she shook her head. Her new career was
progressing nicely and she was proud of her achieve-
ments. She had opted to pull out of her external
university studies this year to concentrate on her
research at the hospital.

But what of your other dreams? the voice taunted.
The research, the travel, the work in Third World
countries you'd always wanted to do?

I can still do that, she assured her unsettled mind.
Eventually!

'Two-hourly check!'

It was the Night Sister herself who came into the
room, and Elly welcomed her. Sitting about in a dimly
lit room provided too much time for unproductive
thoughts! After she had checked Kathryn and written
her observations on the chart, the nurse pulled
the second chair around the bed, and subsided
into it, happy to have an excuse to sit and talk for a
short time.

The remainder of the night passed quickly for Elly,
as the staff on duty dropped in for a chat whenever
they had a few spare minutes. Kathryn did not wake
again until the bustle along the corridors heralded a
change of shift, and the start of another long day.

'Kathryn asked me to phone you and tell you not to
come tonight.'

Sue's call came as Elly was cooking a piece of
chicken for her dinner.

'Is she feeling better or is she tired of my nocturnal vigils?' she asked.

'Feeling much much better,' Sue told her. 'The bandages came off today, and, although there's very little hearing yet, there's no facial paralysis and the surgeon is extremely hopeful. He ordered a lighter dressing, but Kathryn has adopted the board as a favoured means of communication. She hands it to people as they come in, ordering them to "write it down" before they have a chance to go into their pantomime routines.'

'Sounds as if she's much improved,' Elly agreed. 'I can't say I'm sorry about tonight. Three nights without sleep is about as much as I can manage these days. Do you think we find it harder to sleep during the day as we get older.'

'More habit than age,' Sue assured her. 'A long stretch of night-duty would soon sort out that problem.'

Elly chuckled wryly. 'Not for me, thanks,' she protested. 'My biological clock will be happy to get back to normal. See you Monday.'

The weekend stretched before her like a sentence of nothingness. She usually managed to be on duty over the weekend, so that the time when other people played and partied slipped by without her feeling regret or alienation.

With a total lack of interest in the dish she had cooked with such care, she served up her meal and carried it on to the veranda gazing out at the dark water unseeingly, while her mind fought the loneliness that was encroaching faster than she could control it.

Another summons from the phone was a welcome diversion, and she thrust aside the rare mood of self-pity and hurried to answer it.

'As I've finally caught you off-duty on a weekend,

come to dinner tomorrow night,' Sally Jeffs said brightly. 'My kids are all off to camp, so it's an opportunity to have people over without the usual chaos. I'm asking Sue and Bill, Grant Blythe and Maggie, the new ward sister from Maternity, and possibly a couple of other doctors I need to placate. It will be a casual affair—a barbecue, in fact. You know me!'

Elly smiled.

'You mean a casual affair for about fifty people, after you've finished asking half the hospital.'

'Well,' Sally admitted, 'I did ring the Spit Roast people and arrange for them to do the meat and the serving, and I thought I'd order salads from that new deli on the Mall.'

It was half an hour before Elly finally persuaded Sally that the arrangements she had decided on would be ideal.

'Come at five,' Sally told her. 'That way, we can have drinks in the garden before it gets dark.'

Elly agreed, pleased to have something to break up the dreaded weekend, and relieved that a five o'clock start would mean she could leave reasonably early without attracting too much attention. It was enjoyable, seeing other senior staff and the consultants socially on these occasions. Everyone knew each other well enough to make conversation simple and undemanding, and even their usual arguments over pet likes and dislikes held little heat.

'Definitely just what I need,' she told the cat, who didn't appear to care one way or the other!

It must have been the effects of the concussion that had blinded her to this particular possibility, she decided, when she climbed out of the taxi she'd taken to Sally's home and saw the familiar Lexus pull into a spare parking space at the kerb twenty yards along the road.

She hurried through the shrubbery that hid Sally's long, ranch-style home from the road, and followed the sound of music and laughter through the breezeway and out on to the back patio that stretched the length of the house.

Allan Jeffs greeted her with a warm hug and a quick kiss, while friends and colleagues called their welcomes.

'Glass of wine?' Allan asked, and she was about to shake her head when she saw Sally hurry forward to greet the latest arrival. Maybe one glass of wine would make her feel less tense in the new boss's presence.

'Thanks, Allan,' she replied, and looked around for a group of people she could join, as the old saying 'safety in numbers' echoed senselessly in her head.

'You know Elly Winthrop, of course!'

Escape was too late! Sally was bearing down on her like a little tug with a very big ship in tow. The unfortunate Dr Ballantyne, unable to escape the hand that gripped his arm so tenaciously, was following her with a martyred expression on his dark face.

'Sister Winthrop!'

He bowed formally towards her, and her eyes caught a slight twitching movement at the corner of his lips, as if he was trying hard to control a rueful smile.

'Dr Ballantyne,' she returned, equally formally, determining to get away from him as soon as possible. Surely he must realise she had as little wish for his company as he apparently had for hers!

'For heaven's sake, you two,' Sally expostulated. 'It's Gregor and Elly. You can't be the only people at my party sticking to hospital protocol.'

Gregor. I like that, Elly decided, and looked up at

him to match the name to his face.

'Hello, Elly,' he said, with a slight smile, and the sound of the words reminded her fleetingly of black velvet, although she couldn't fathom how such a ridiculous notion had come into her head.

'You're supposed to say, "Hello Gregor,"' he told her, with such sweet sincerity that she peered suspiciously at his deadpan face to see if she could detect a teasing gleam of humour or a hint of his more usual sarcasm.

Her lips refused to form the words, but Allan's arrival with her glass of wine saved her, and she thanked him effusively then watched him lead 'Gregor' over to the bar to view the non-alcoholic beverages on offer.

Seeing Sue's husband, Bill, on the fringe of one cluster of people, she hurried off, attaching herself to him with the relief of a limpet finding a rock in a storm-tossed sea.

'Do you mind if I cling a little, Bill?' she asked, and was rewarded by the warmth of his arm slipping round her waist and drawing her close against his side.

'Still feeling fragile?' he asked, looking anxiously at her face.

'A little,' she admitted, but didn't add that it was more to do with the company than the concussion.

'It was a dreadful thing,' he went on, his loud voice drawing the others' attention to her presence, and prompting a chorus of sympathetic enquiries and heated denunciations of the lighting in the car park.

Brushing off the concern, she listened to the banter and chuckled as the suggestions for protecting staff in the car park grew increasingly outrageous.

Gregor heard the deep, gurgling notes of her laughter as he crossed the patio with Allan. While his ears

registered the attractiveness of the sound, his eyes were
on the tall slim figure, not beautiful, but attractive in
the way of an unusual work of art.

Did she dress to enhance her difference? he
wondered, taking in the long, slender legs encased in
navy leggings, and the brightly coloured, knitted top
that was either a long pullover or an abbreviated dress.
The swirling blue, green and purple in the top made
her stand out like a peacock in a flock of sparrows,
for the other women, and most of the men, were uni-
formly dressed in cream, brown, beige or grey trousers,
with an occasional flash of a red sweater, but a pre-
dominance of the same colours covering their top
halves.

He had been wondering at his own choice of black
trousers and a long-sleeved but casual black and white
silk shirt, until he saw her vivid brightness. I admire
your style and the spirit it must take to carry it through,
Ellen Winthrop, he admitted silently, despite the fact
I'm not one hundred per cent certain about your
humanity towards anyone other than your patients.
And the contrast between your on-duty personality and
the. . .'insouciance' is the only word I can find—of
your home and clothing is a further puzzle!

There was another burst of laughter from the group,
and he looked again, wondering who the man was.
The almost palpable intensity of a lover was absent in
the casual way the man's arm was slung around her
waist, but Gregor found himself resenting the man's
attitude, deploring the stranger's closeness to that
abrasive female he barely knew!

'Do you know Sue Childs?' Allan was saying, and
he dragged his mind away from its distracting thoughts
and smiled a greeting at the shift sister he had briefly
met during his initial appointments with senior staff.

Elly's confidence evaporated as she heard Sue's voice behind her, exhorting Gregor to join their group and meet her husband. She could hardly dart away and attach herself to another friend's husband, nor could she wander off, and draw attention to herself by standing alone.

Sue introduced him into the gathering with the triumphant aplomb of a magician producing a pigeon from a handkerchief, and the conversation heightened as the new arrival was included. People made the appropriate noises of welcome and enquiries about his reaction to the hospital, the city of the Gold Coast and the balmy winter weather.

'How are you feeling?' he asked, turning directly to her when the focus of attention switched away from him.

'I'm fine,' she lied, wondering why she should be suffering such physical uncertainty right now when she knew she was well over the effects of her concussion. Her stomach was clenched into a tight knot, and she could feel a trembly sensation in her limbs, as if her bones were dissolving into a frothy mass of nothingness.

'You're certainly looking much better,' he said, and she wondered, much better than what? as he added a quiet, 'Those colours suit you, but then, so did that pinky orange thing you were wearing the other day.'

'Compliments, Dr Ballantyne?' she asked coolly, and hoped to cover the confusion his words had caused with a false little laugh. He had not struck her as a man given to social chit-chat and meaningless tributes.

'Stating a fact,' he told her, his face still unsmiling as he looked hard into her eyes. 'I doubt you'd accept anything else, particularly not from me!'

Now what did the man mean by that? she wondered desperately.

'Kathryn's much better,' she mumbled, dismayed that his expressionless scrutiny was unnerving her to the point where she was almost shaking. She was pleased her knitted top had long sleeves, for she was certain there were goose-bumps on her skin, visible signs of her reaction to the man.

'So you've stopped your nightly vigil?'

'Quite thankfully,' she admitted, as Grant Blythe came up to them with his wife, and a neurosurgeon, Clive Evans, who had been on the Coast for less than twelve months.

She spoke to Maggie, turning aside the anxious enquiries about her health.

'For someone supposedly at death's door, you're looking remarkably healthy,' Clive remarked, and Elly restricted her reply to a shrug and a slight smile. Clive had asked her out repeatedly when he first arrived, but there was something about his attitude that rubbed Elly the wrong way, and she had kindly but firmly refused his offers.

'Be good to have you back; the place is chaotic without you,' he continued, only half joking, and the irritation she invariably felt in his presence flared up again.

'You're usually telling me how chaotic it is under my direction,' she said tartly, and then sensed the quick glance the new hospital owner sent in her direction.

Damn Clive for bringing up shop-talk, she thought, annoyed both with him and with herself for hitting back at him.

'I have to tell you that to keep you in your place, my dear,' he retorted, before turning to speak to Gregor with the air of an old acquaintance.

Elly dragged air into her lungs, forcing herself to relax. Maggie and Sue discussed childcare problems on one side of her, while Clive and Gregor Ballantyne played the, 'Whatever happened to so-and-so?' game on the other. It was Clive who mentioned a 'Josie' but whatever he had hoped to find out from the query was lost as Gregor countered not with a reply about the unknown female but with a deliberate, 'Did you know Ellen is old Prof Winthrop's daughter?' and all the air she'd carefully absorbed left her lungs in a gasping rush.

'Why ever didn't you tell me that?' Clive was asking as she tried to regather her senses. The aggrieved way he spoke suggested they were closer personal friends than was, in fact, the truth, and this added to her discomfort.

'I think Sister Winthrop tries to keep it quiet. Not one to bask in the old man's reflected glory, I suspect,' her tormentor responded for her, a thread of something like contempt running through the cynical remark.

'I tell people who ask,' she responded quietly, unwilling to put up with the unprovoked baiting this man seemed to enjoy at her expense.

'He lives here on the Coast,' Gregor Ballantyne persisted. 'Perhaps we should call in and see him one day.'

'Not me, thanks,' Clive said quickly. The old man never did think much of my ability. I wouldn't want to cop any further denigration of my efforts at this stage of my life. You, of course, were always the teacher's pet. You go and visit him.'

Elly chewed at her lower lip, watching the to and fro of the conversation like a spectator at a tennis match.

'I might just do that!' The words came out in a slow drawl, and Gregor looked, not at Clive as he spoke, but directly down at her.

She felt the blood drain out of her face, and a sick churning of her stomach made her regret the wine, but she met his eyes and held them, determined not to betray the anguish he was causing her.

'My father has Alzheimer's,' she said, hoping her voice was not shaking as badly as the rest of her appeared to be. 'It would be a kind gesture on your part to visit him, but that is all it would be. If you expect him to remember you, or to hold a learned discussion on neurone synapses, then you will be disappointed.'

Without waiting to see the effect of her words on her audience, she turned and walked away, setting down her empty glass on a convenient window ledge, before heading back through the breezeway towards the road.

Her legs were stiff and uncoordinated, as if the messages from her brain had become distorted. The grief she had contained when her father's forgetfulness had forced a realisation of his illness upon her pressed down on her shoulders, and the tears she had not shed when he deteriorated far more rapidly than his doctor had anticipated now flowed so freely that the footpath shimmered beneath her feet.

She would ring Sally later and plead a sudden overwhelming tiredness, she comforted herself as she stumbled along, head bent to hide the tears she could not stop. She could blame the concussion; Sally would understand! The depression that had been hovering round the edges of her life descended on her like a thick black cloud and she moved through it with little conscious recognition of where she was, or what she was doing.

A jolt as strong as an electric shock had struck Gregor when he saw the colour leave her face, making the sprinkle of gold freckles stand out like a strange rash across her nose and cheeks. But it was the depth of the anguish in the simple diagnostic statement that had shaken him the most, a rare compassion squeezing at his heart like a giant hand.

And *he* had forced her to say the words that had hurt her so much! She'd shut him off once before when he'd mentioned her father, but had he taken the hint? Oh, no! He'd had to make his own judgements. His great mind had decided she was resentful, or, worse still, ashamed of the fact that her father was an invalid. He'd written her off as an efficient machine, geared to provide the best possible service with the least possible cost to her ordered sensibilities.

The pain in her abrupt confession had been real enough! It had knocked her for six—and had not done him much good either, he decided, trying to gather his senses as he watched her walk away, her shoulders hunched forward protectively as if to prevent further pain.

By the time he'd recovered sufficiently to figure out that she wasn't coming back on to the patio, and had searched the house unsuccessfully, he was furious. With himself for upsetting her with his insistence, and with her, for making him feel the way he did. He'd seen her arrive in a taxi, but was reasonably certain she hadn't had time to phone one before he started his search.

Without excusing himself to his hostess, he hurried out to his car, and saw the small figure in the distance, still moving doggedly away from the house.

She seemed unaware of her surroundings, as she moved, one foot in front of the other, with an automation that frightened him.

'Hop in!' he ordered, pushing open the passenger side door, as his car glided to a halt beside her.

She stopped and turned, raising both her hands to her face as she did so, and wiping away the seeping moisture with her fingers, like a child who needed to see what was being offered as a comfort.

The hand squeezed at his heart again, as he saw the blankness of shock in her face, and the defeated droop of her shoulders.

Opening his own door, he clambered out and moved swiftly to her side, sliding an arm around her shoulders, and holding her close for a moment.

'I'll drive you home,' he said, calmly and quietly, urging her unresponsive body towards the car.

Relief overwhelmed him when she moved. It was like being given a second chance at something very important, something he had already bungled with disastrous results.

She subsided into the seat, and he pulled the seat belt free and leaned down to strap it around her, shocked by the apathy of this woman who had stood up to him from their first encounter.

'Tell me about it,' he said, quietly but firmly as he sank down into his own seat and closed the door. His finely tuned diagnostic skill sensed that the time was right for her to talk.

'He continued with his research when he retired,' she said, rubbing a handkerchief across her face to remove the last trace of the tears he could still hear in her voice. 'Retired down here to the Coast, and kept in touch by computer with various institutes and specialist magazines.'

He watched her regain the physical strength that some form of delayed shock had drained from her bones, seeing the slight straightening of her shoulders, the determined raising of her stubborn chin. He gave a silent cheer, admitting and admiring a courage he believed was very rare.

'Because he was using the computer, the signs were, at first, unnoticeable.'

She looked at him now, as if wondering how much he wanted to know, or how much he was absorbing. Her green eyes were the colour of the palest fringe of the sea, a magical translucent green seen only in photos of untouched tropical islands where it washed over coral reefs to a white beach.

'Hand-eye co-ordination is usually the first physical sign—trouble with written words, with getting a signature to look the same every time you write it. Memory dysfunction is usually put down to age-related forgetfulness, until other symptoms become apparent.'

He nodded, professionally pleased by the evenness of her voice, personally enjoying the soft cadence of it.

'I lived, studied and worked in Brisbane, coming down when I was off duty. I had finished my training and degree course and was doing post graduate study to become a nurse-educator. Then, he was diagnosed with cancer of the colon.'

The words had a dispassionate matter-of-factness, as if they had been rehearsed over and over again before this telling.

'Medically speaking, he came through the operation with an amazing facility for a man in his eighties, and physically he recovered quickly. Mentally. . .' She shrugged, and turned to look out the window. Her fingers pressed against the glass, as if they were trying to escape the imprisonment of her emotions.

'There's been some work done on the effects of anaesthesia on the elderly, but not enough specifically targeting Alzheimer's patients. Whether it is a general effect, or was specific to my father, I don't know,' she told him with a calmness he was certain she did not feel, 'but his mental condition deteriorated rapidly after the operation, to the stage where he is now almost entirely oblivious of everything except changes in his routine.'

And my distress, she thought, but did not say.

CHAPTER SIX

'It's appalling to think of that happening to such a fine brain,' he said gruffly.

Elly shifted in her seat, settling her head back at an angle so she could look at him, but he was turning the key in the car's ignition, and she was presented with a strongly angled profile, and the flat plane of his cheek. Neither gave the remotest hint of his mood or feelings!

'Your friends must know of his condition.' It was a statement, not a question, but the quick, searching glance that accompanied the words made her nod her agreement.

'They know he has Alzheimer's,' she said flatly. 'To them it is a diagnosis, not a reality. They have sufficient understanding of the disease to feel pity for me, and absolutely no notion of what it entails to live with on a daily basis.'

She turned away and looked out the window, watching familiar landmarks flash past. They were not heading for her home, but she was beyond caring. The tide of emotion that had swept over her so unexpectedly had washed away all her energy, and she was content to sit and be driven.

'And you'd rather have a little more understanding and a little less pity?'

He sounded clinically interested, and she found she could cope with that.

'I certainly don't want pity, and the understanding of the practical side is already there. Sally starting the

97

party early tonight, for example,' she told him. 'She knows I like to be home by ten—it's part of a routine I try to keep. The problem is that it's something you have to experience to fully understand.'

They were heading out towards the Spit, a long, narrow stretch of land between the sheltered waters of the Broadwater and the wide golden surfing beach that was one of the attractions of the Gold Coast. She was unperturbed, her body filled with an unfamiliar lassitude, while her mind searched for words to explain her feelings about her father's illness.

'In fact,' she added, 'I'm not certain that actually living with it brings understanding. It's such an irrational thing, and there's always the underlying dread that he is suffering more because he knows he's lost something as precious as the ability to think.'

'How advanced is it?'

He still didn't look at her, all his concentration on the narrow road that led to the Seaway, where a long rock wall stretched out to provide a protected entrance for boats entering or leaving the Broadwater.

'It's hard to tell,' she admitted, not knowing whether to feel ashamed or defensive. 'I could find out more if he had a brain scan to assess the extent of the damage, and subsequent scans to follow the deterioration, but he is unsettled in strange places. . .'

She paused, remembering the times she'd argued with herself about this option. 'It's hard to justify putting him through any discomfort to satisfy my own curiosity,' she finally confessed.

Her chauffeur slid the car into a patch of shade beneath a clump of drooping casuarina trees, and, as he turned off the ignition, he swung around to face her, looking across the small space between them with an unreadable expression on his face.

'You're something of an enigma, Sister Winthrop,' he said at last, then reached down between the seats for a small mobile phone.

Elly watched him, unsettled by a sudden shift in the atmosphere in the small, enclosed space. A long bony finger jabbed at the numbers, and she saw the misshapen joint, but rejected the flare of sympathy. Pity wasn't something this man would want, she acknowledged.

'Sally? Gregor Ballantyne. Sorry to dash off like that but Ellen wasn't feeling well and I offered to drive her home. I thought it better to slip away quietly than make a fuss,' Elly heard him say, smoothing over the lie with social niceness.

The encapsulating confines of the car seemed to shrink, and an uneasiness that had nothing to do with the conversation began to creep over her. It was as if her nerve-endings had suddenly become aware of the man, seeking out and reacting to the invisible, yet distinctly masculine, magnetic field that surrounded him. She tried to concentrate on what he was saying in an attempt to distract her brain from the messages her skin was sending to it.

Sally must have asked him to come back and eat with them, for he added, 'No, some other time, maybe,' before thanking her politely and disconnecting.

'If you drop me back at the Mirage, I can take a taxi home, and you'll still be able to get back for dinner,' Elly told him firmly, suddenly aware of the extent to which she had disrupted Sally's party. 'You were probably the unofficial guest of honour,' she added as the awful truth dawned on her. 'She would have asked all those people so you could meet them socially.'

'There's been no shortage of social invitations,' he responded drily. Then his hand reached out and touched her arm. 'Are you up to a walk? I discovered the sea-wall when I was lost one day. It's a great place to walk when your head needs clearing—enough breeze to blow any sticky cobwebs away.'

'Enough breeze to blow the hair off your head, more likely,' she told him tartly, but the idea was appealing and she was already opening the car door.

Good manners decreed that he put out a hand to help her over the rocks that led up onto the smooth path on the top of the wall, but a reluctance to have her reject his offer made him hesitate, and he missed his opportunity. She was ahead of him, the wind she'd foretold teasing at her braided hair so that tendrils of it blew around her face, striping the pale skin with fine lines of colour.

The sun had disappeared behind the mountains, but the bright glow of its departure still lingered in the western sky, lighting the still waters to a molten gold. Turning their backs on the flagrant beauty of a day that seemed reluctant to end, they walked out to where the surf battered itself tirelessly against the wall, sending fine bursts of water upwards like an erratic fountain.

She moved with a brisk, long-legged stride that matched his effortlessly, and he discovered a sense of peace in her company that he realised had been missing from his life for a long time.

Elly felt the wind tearing at her hair, and revelled in the crispness of it in her lungs. Out here, she was free, relieved of all concerns and constraints.

'I must go sailing again,' she said, the words colliding with his,

'Will you have dinner with me tonight?'

Elly halted and turned to look at him, as much surprised by her own sudden decision as she was by his invitation.

'I think that would be stretching the story you've already told Sally just a little too far,' she said cautiously, although the invitation had sifted into a hidden place in her heart that had been empty for too long.

He shrugged, but did not speak, and the silence stretched between them with a tension that was strangely physical. Elly was aware of that tall, bulky body with an intensity that frightened, and yet excited her.

'I could offer you a steak and salad at my place,' she said, and heard the words whipped away by the wind so quickly she wondered if they had reached him.

For an infinitesimal space of time she thought he was going to ignore her, but his body had swayed closer and was bombarding hers with messages she could not misinterpret. Panic flared, then died down again, as he nodded his head, and replied, 'That would be delightful, thank you, Sister Winthrop.'

They turned to walk back to the car, the words of acceptance echoing in Elly's head. Had the formal response been deliberate? His way of telling her that theirs was a purely professional relationship? But she knew that! A man like this would see nothing in a plain woman like herself. And besides, there was Debbie! And who knew how many other women?

A man like this probably projected his sexuality unconsciously, yet had enough experience to know when a woman reacted to it. He was putting her off, in the kindest possible way, she decided. Not that she was interested anyway.

She found herself shrinking into her own space, walking stiffly now, lest her sleeve accidentally brush against his, or a swinging hand feel the warmness of his skin.

The phone was ringing when they reached the car, and she walked a few yards away, unwilling to eaves-drop on his private conversation. The name 'Josie' reached her clearly enough, and she remembered hearing it earlier in the afternoon and wondered idly who it was.

Then he was by her side, so close she could feel the warmth emanating from him. He slipped an arm around her shoulders, as he had done earlier when he'd led her to his car. Yet this time he hesitated, and they both stood, hip to hip, watching the last remnants of colour fade from the water and a deep enveloping darkness settle over the scene.

'I'll run you home,' he said at last, 'but I'm afraid I'll have to cry off dinner. A—' he hesitated, as if unsure of the right word, then finished with a strained composure '—friend of mine has been hospitalised in Brisbane. I'll have to drive up there tonight.'

'That's quite all right,' she told him briskly. If he wanted Sister Winthrop, he could have her. 'I was feeling a bit weary anyway. Night duty never did agree with me.'

She would have liked to say more, liked to thank him for listening to her, for making her talk about things she'd kept bottled up inside her since her father's deterioration began, but the words belonged to Elly, the emotional, confused, silly woman who had reacted to him as a man, when all he considered himself to be was her boss.

Damn Jocee, he thought savagely as he backed the car out of the parking space and turned it back along the narrow road. He had begun to think he was breaking

through the barrier of reserve the woman wore like a
suit of armour when one phone call had disrupted
everything. It was like drawing the Go to Jail card at
Monopoly, he decided frustratedly, and now he was
back to square one, for there was no mistaking the
return of the starchy ward sister in the calm acceptance
of his excuse.

And the car was too damn small! He could feel her
there beside him like a crackling fire, radiating that
strange, strong, seductive sexuality instead of heat.
Surely she must be conscious of it, and aware of his
response to it!

To Elly, the atmosphere in the car tightened, as if all
the air had been sucked out and they were left sus-
pended in a vacuum. She sat rigidly in her seat as he
drove, with an impatient haste, towards her home.
Every movement spelt out his anxiety, his desire to be
rid of her and on his way to Brisbane.

'I'm sorry to have inconvenienced you like this, but
you can get back on to the Brisbane road by going
over Hope Island,' she told him, pointing up along the
road that had brought them out to Hollywell.

'I'm the one who should be apologising,' he replied
brusquely, but he didn't elaborate, and she was left
wondering what he meant. The car pulled up outside
her house and she slid swiftly out with a jumbled
stammering of thanks and apologies.

'I'll catch up with you during the week,' was all he
said, but he did not drive off until she had unlocked
her door, and was walking into the brightly lit foyer.

Elly returned to work with a sense of relief. Ignoring
the exhortations of the new owner, she drove, knowing
that she was mentally fit enough and determined to

face the bogey of the car park at the earliest opportunity.

'Mayhem in this place at present,' the shift sister greeted her cheerfully. 'I doubt even your strong hands back on the reins will pull it into shape this week!'

'Perhaps I should take another week off,' she suggested, only half joking as a curious reluctance to see Gregor Ballantyne again had been building up within her since Saturday night.

'Don't you dare,' came a warning cry, and she turned to see Grant Blythe coming in for an early ward round. 'I've a carotid endarterectomy coming in this morning, for surgery at crack of dawn tomorrow. I wanted him in early to see if you could calm him down before the operation. He's a big wheel in business here on the Coast, and is one of those chaps who thinks that because he's king of his own little world he's the king of everywhere. Needs careful handling, kind but firm.'

'His medical background might be more useful than these dire warnings.'

Grant grinned at her acidic remark.

'He's had a series of transient ischemic attacks which took him too long to recognise as signs of something being wrong. Fancy a man losing sight in one eye, or the feeling in a hand, and not doing something about it. He often felt dizzy and put it down to tiredness.'

'Is he hypertensive?' Elly asked.

'What high-powered businessman in his late forties isn't? He's been on various blood-pressure remedies from his local doctor, who also hadn't been told about the dizzy spells and transitory loss of sight!'

He sounded so disgusted, Elly had to grin.

'I bet you told him just how stupid he was when he finally made it to your rooms!'

'Well, he was!' Grant protested. 'TIA's can be successfully treated by surgery to prevent recurrences and reduce the risk of stroke, if only patients will get to us before it's too late.'

'And now you're passing this problem patient over to me?'

'Anyone but you in charge, and he'll have the whole hospital reorganised around his wishes and commands.'

'Thanks, friend!' Elly said, a smile tugging at her lips in appreciation of the hidden compliment.

'You'll handle him,' Grant reiterated confidently, 'providing you're fit, of course.' He peered closely at her, and Elly realised that it was probably the first time within the hospital walls that Grant had looked at her as a person.

'I'm fine,' she told him, but his scrutiny continued for longer than was necessary, and, when he finally nodded she imagined it was a confirmation, not of her health, but of something else.

'So that's one potential problem,' she said, turning back to the records as he left the desk. 'What else have you got for me?'

'I didn't know about that one,' the night sister told her, ruefully shaking her head as she foresaw the problems an autocratic patient could cause. 'We've already got one little despot. Admitted yesterday, she's in Fourteen. Wanted a bed swap immediately she arrived, according to Sue who was on the split shift and admitted her.'

'Sounds a real treat! Who's she under?'

'That's what's odd about it! She's had reconstruction surgery—coronal, mid and lower face, and upper neck, with liposuction of jowl and and submental regions— but it was done in Brisbane, and she was transferred down to us. We're assuming she'll be under Dr Brown here, but the admission forms were signed by Dr Ballantyne himself.'

'Presumably, as he owns the hospital, he can admit whoever he likes,' Elly responded tartly as a sharp pain pierced her lungs and made breathing difficult. This must be the 'friend' he had dashed up to Brisbane to see, the decision to move her made for his own convenience.

The night sister nodded, then continued down the list of patients, adding a comment now and then.

'Kathryn's doing really well, and definitely has some hearing, at this early stage. She's a joy to nurse as she's so determined to be well again as soon as possible.'

'Give me a positive patient any day,' Elly agreed, making a mental note of the nurses she would have on duty and deciding on the distribution of the new patients among them. The day had begun, and she welcomed the familiarity of the routine.

Until Debbie appeared at the desk, a mutinous look on her usually cheerful face!

'I won't do Fourteen,' she announced, hiding an unspoken distress under a bluntness that was unusual in her.

'"Won't", Nurse Morrison?' Elly responded in her best 'sister-in-charge' manner. She watched the young woman closely as she spoke and saw her try to control whatever emotion was stirring within her before she spoke again.

'I would prefer not to, please, Sister,' she said more mildly, and it appeared to Elly that pride or anger, or a mixture of both, was forbidding her to beg. She should insist the nurse accept the patient allocated to her—that was the established policy and wards ran well when you followed it—but personal disagreements or antipathy between a patient and nurse could cause havoc and seriously disrupt the patient's recovery. She consulted the lists.

'Fifteen will be discharged this morning and has a new admission coming in late morning. See Anne Forbes about it. I'm sure she'd be willing to swap.'

'Thanks, Sister!' Debbie said gratefully, moving away in search of Anne before Elly had time to question her reluctance to nurse the patient in Room Fourteen, or change her mind about the switch.

Elly watched her go. She would be doing a ward round shortly, to say hello to all the patients in her care. Should she start with Fourteen, or leave her till last?

Gregor Ballantyne's arrival put a stop to speculation. With a curt nod towards the desk, which encompassed herself, the departing sister and the ward clerk, he continued on his way, entering Fourteen after the lightest of taps on the door.

Was some stupid personal jealousy behind Debbie's refusal to do Fourteen? Was Gregor Ballantyne causing problems she didn't need on her ward?

She fought the anger her thoughts had provoked, and started her round with the double rooms. She'd go on to the four-bed wards, and hope he'd be gone by the time she reached the singles and the unknown patient in Fourteen. She was pleased with her decision, but some of the contentment of her return to work had been dimmed by his cursory greeting, and his presence within the place she considered her personal domain caused a disruptive feeling that was as unfamiliar as it was uncomfortable.

As the day gathered momentum, she set aside the inauspicious beginning, and gathered up the invisible strings that tied her to the patients. The woman in

Fourteen greeted her with a bored indifference, merely asking her to renew the ice-packs she had resting on her eyes. She was on the patient-controlled analgesics, Elly noted, and reminded herself to add her to the list in her research.

Jacqueline Olivia Craig was her name, Elly discovered, reading through the notes while Anne went for ice-packs. The surgeon who had performed the operation had signed her out of a private hospital in Brisbane, and included all her particulars with the discharge. Unusual, but not unheard of, Elly admitted to herself.

She was debating whether to discuss the hospital move with the patient when the ward clerk signalled to her from the door. 'The MRI machine has blown a fuse or something, so Dr Evans' patient won't be going down at eleven,' Alison murmured as she came out into the corridor. 'They've rescheduled him for three this afternoon.'

Clive's patient had been admitted as an emergency, with muscle weakness, bowel and bladder disturbances, impaired memory and judgement and non-fluent aphasia. They were classic symptoms of a frontal lobe tumour, and it was imperative to get him into the magnetic resonance imaging machine as quickly as possible.

The size and position of the tumour, indicated by the machine, would dictate the next stage of treatment, and, as always, she had uttered a silent prayer that it would be a meningioma, not a glioblastoma. The chances of the patient's survival after complete surgical removal of meningioma were high.

Right now, though, there was nothing she could do.

'That's OK', Elly assured her. 'I'll just check whether he was to have any pre-med, and alter the time for that as well. Phone Dr Evans and let him know of the delay.'

Out of the corner of her eye, she saw the light come on above Fourteen's door as she went back to the desk. Anne had barely had time to leave the room before she was being called back. Elly sighed, understanding what the shift sister had meant about a despot.

And Alexander Walsh promised to be worse, she decided an hour later, as she tried to convince him that a large slug of Scotch was not quite what his doctor had in mind when he spoke of drinking more liquids.

'I'm taking that bottle, and if necessary will give orders for your visitors to be strip searched before they go into your room,' she told him firmly. 'You may have a glass of wine with your lunch, but too much alcohol in your blood could lead to problems both during and after your operation,' she added calmly, ignoring the fierce frown in his blue eyes.

'It's a simple operation and I'll only be in for a few days, Dr Blythe told me,' he argued, standing up so they were eye to eye.

'It's a simple operation if all goes well,' she responded, 'so stop glowering at me and accept the fact that in here people jump to my command not yours.'

Much to her relief, he sat down again, laughing loudly at his defeat. She was pleased the tough standover tactics had worked, probably because it was the way he operated himself.

'Leave the Scotch, I won't drink it,' he told her, reaching out for the bottle.

'I'd prefer not to take the risk,' she told him. 'And who knows who'd you'd be offering it to if I leave it here!'

'You'd be the first,' he said, and something in his

voice alerted Ellen to a change in his mood. He was smiling at her in a strange way. Surely he couldn't be flirting with her? She shook her head and excused herself. Debbie would be able to manage him—after all, she seemed to be attracted to older men.

'Mrs Craig wants a stronger pain-killer,' Anne greeted her as she left the room.

'Has one of our consultants taken over the case?' Elly asked, pausing outside the door of Fourteen and speaking quietly.

'No. Dr Ballantyne signed for the dosage she's on, and the approval for patient control. I'm wondering if she opted for it thinking she could have as much as she liked,' Anne said in a worried voice. 'She might not have known about the lock-out intervals that prevent overdosing.'

'She can't have more than is prescribed,' Elly said tartly, wondering if her annoyance with the woman would be as strong if it weren't for the disruptive personal influences at work in the ward.

'I'll see her,' she added with a wry resignation.

'I'm in a lot of pain,' the woman moaned, her lips painted a bright pink, and the visible bits of her face looking quite serene and unaffected by her agony! 'I think the nurse has forgotten to put the medication into this machine.'

'Do you know what doctor will be looking after you down here?' Elly asked, stifling an urge to tell her to stop complaining. Cosmetic surgery was elective, after all!

'Why, Gregor will, of course,' the woman said, her tone conveying how stupid she considered the question.

The assumption puzzled Elly. She supposed the owner of a hospital, if a doctor, could prescribe for a patient, but it was a new situation and she was uncertain how to tackle it.

'I'll speak to Dr Ballantyne,' was all she said, as she walked out of the room, noting with a peculiar twist of humour that the woman wasn't in too much pain to lift the receiver of the phone by her bed.

Back at the desk Clive Evans was berating Alison about his patient who hadn't received his prescribed sedative.

'The equipment is off-line and the MRI has been re-scheduled for three o'clock,' Elly told him sharply. 'We phoned through to your rooms to let you know, but you must have missed the message,' she added, and was pleased to see he looked quite shamefaced, and surprised to hear a mumbled apology fall from his lips before he swept away.

'See if you can get Dr Ballantyne on the phone, and tell him I'd like to speak to him about Mrs Craig's medication,' she told Alison, before hurrying off in response to a cry for the key.

'Welcome back to normal chaos, huh?' one of her senior nurses asked as they passed in the corridor a little later, and Elly had to grin, a reaction that was quickly wiped away when she saw a glowering Gregor Ballantyne bearing down on her.

'I'd like to see you for a moment in the interview-room,' he said, repressed fury emanating from every line in his taut body. She turned and followed him into the little room, feeling a distress that was unconnected with her normal professional attitude.

'Two complaints in one morning are a bit much to gloss over, even considering the fact you've been on sick leave,' he said sharply, looking out the window into the shady courtyard and tossing the words over his shoulder at her.

'Two complaints, Dr Ballantyne?' she asked as coolly as she could manage, with her heart beating like a trip-hammer and a sick disappointment gnawing at her stomach.

'Two,' he reiterated nastily. 'I was on my way to see one patient about a complaint when Clive Evans pulled me up in the passage and gave me a ten-minute harangue about the inefficiency of this ward. Does a pre-med he'd specifically ordered ring any bells in that supposedly efficient head of yours?'

The sneering sarcasm of the man was unbelievable after his consideration only two days earlier. Was he afraid he had let down some imaginary guard the other evening? Was this overplayed reaction a result of some weakness he perceived in his behaviour or some irrational concern that she might take advantage of his kindness? His back view told her nothing!

'Dr Evans' office was advised that his patient's MRI had been rescheduled, but the message did not reach him,' she told him, keeping her voice steady although her temper was rising again. This man could produce more emotions in her in five minutes than the most extreme soap opera could portray in a half-hour episode. 'There was little point in giving the man a sedative at eleven for a procedure that was not to take place until three this afternoon. I have since seen Dr Evans and explained this.'

Not that he had admitted he'd gone running to the boss with his tale! she thought, as she stood there, impatient to get back to her work, but not willing to prompt him to further abuse.

As she watched the rigid back, she saw some of the tension drain out of it, and a visible relaxation in his shoulders. Had the hands she knew would be clenched in his pockets relaxed as well? she wondered, remembering, with a touch of sympathy, their gnarled shape.

He turned to face her, and she hoped he hadn't caught a glimpse of her feeling in her face. Not a man to welcome sympathy, she divined.

'Mrs Craig tells me you're refusing to give her pain-killers,' he continued, a new hesitancy in his voice suggesting that he was now unsure of the validity of this other claim, and somewhat embarrassed by his earlier anger.

'The ward clerk has been trying to get hold of you to ask about her medication. She's receiving the amount prescribed on her chart but is asking for more.' She would have liked to add, 'And you know very well that we can't give anything stronger than aspirin or Panadol without a doctor's authority,' but sensed a rare uncertainty in the man that made her refrain from pushing her point.

'It must make you feel good to see me in the wrong,' he muttered, and she could feel his discomfort as if it was a physical presence in the room, niggling at her own sensitivity and making her shrug uncomfortably.

'Why should it?' she asked and watched him turn away from her again, as if the view outside the window was infinitely more inviting than her face. 'They could have been quite legitimate complaints and you'd hardly have been doing your job if you'd ignored them.'

His refusal to look at her roused her anger, and she added crisply, 'Although it might have been more sensible to listen to both sides of the story before making judgements.'

'You're right, of course,' he said, so quietly that the expected sense of righteous victory failed to lighten Elly's mood. 'I'll see Mrs Craig and let you know about her medication.'

Hearing her own dismissal in the words, Elly left, her bewilderment over the man's behaviour accentuated by her own erratic reactions to it.

'Fifteen's demanding your immediate attention,' an orderly told her as she emerged, and she switched her mind away from Dr Gregor Ballantyne, and sighed as she prepared to tackle the man who would make all their lives as difficult as possible for the next few days, if she couldn't get him under control.

'Yes, Mr Walsh,' she said in her most brisk professional manner as she swept through the door into his room.

'I understood nurses were supposed to hold my hand and pat my fevered brow,' he said plaintively, and underneath the jocularity she recognised an apprehension a man like this would never admit. 'I'm left here all alone for hours on end, and when I ring the bell, that pretty child whisks in and out so quickly I haven't a chance to even grab at her skirt.'

Elly suppressed a smile.

'It's a special technique we're taught during our training,' she said with a straight face. 'Lectures Ten and Eleven, usually! Evading the Grip of the Groper, and Punishing the Ploys of the Persistent Pincher!'

His laughter, whole-hearted and good to hear, shook the bed.

'You're all sadists,' he grumbled. 'I'm lonely! Can't you sit and talk for a bit.'

It was as close as this man would ever get to admitting his fear, she realised, and she responded with a warm smile.

'I'll check on the latest crisis out there, and come back on my lunch break,' she promised, then added with a grin, 'We can exchange thoughts on how to terrify our underlings while we eat.'

Gregor Ballantyne was the most obvious crisis, hovering by the desk with impatience eddying from his fingertips as they danced on the desk.

'I'd like to see you about Mrs Craig, Sister,' he said as she approached. 'Perhaps you could join me for a cup of coffee in your lunch break.'

Honestly, she thought, the man is as unpredictable as a bucket of sky-rockets all set off at once. One minute he's blazing away at me for supposed misdemeanours, and the next asking me to lunch so he can talk to me about his own pet patient.

'I've arranged to lunch with someone,' she told him, and saw the quick anger flicker in his eyes before the careful mask of indifference fell back into place.

'Maybe later, then,' was all he said, striding away from her as if he was personally affronted by her behaviour.

CHAPTER SEVEN

Clive Evans accompanied his patient back up from Radiography, and stopped by the desk.

'Sorry if I got you into strife with the new boss,' he said, with a smooth false smile that made Elly want to hit him.

'You sound it!' she responded waspishly. 'And a lot of good saying sorry is when he's already bawled me out over it!'

The object of her anger remained unabashed, merely commenting, 'I suppose you'll have him hanging round the place all day, with the precious Jocee in your ward.'

'Josie?'

'Jocee Carr, or Ballantyne, or Craig as she is now,' he explained, but Elly was still lost.

'Mrs Craig's name is Jacqueline,' she muttered feebly, trying to sort through the confusion that had reduced her mind to a ball of fluff.

'That's still Jocee,' Clive told her with a certain maliciousness in his voice. 'Jacqueline Olivia Carr she was originally, with the initials J. O. C., or Jo C. That, of course, was before Gregor snapped her up, and she became J. O. B. I doubt if she ever liked the change of her own special initials, but the Ballantynes had plenty of money and——'

'I don't like gossip, Clive, nor do I think it's the kind of talk you should be spreading round the hospital.' Elly interrupted the flow with her acerbic comment, and watched, without regret, as Clive shrugged a farewell and left.

Gossip was endemic in a hospital, but it wasn't something she had ever encouraged, or spread. Yet the words had been spoken and her foggy mind would not let them go. If there was something going on between Gregor Ballantyne and Debbie, it explained the young woman's reluctance to nurse Mrs Craig. But if Number Fourteen's name had been Carr and was now Craig, then there must have been another husband since Gregor Ballantyne. So why would he be expected to haunt the place? Unless he was still in love with her. . . .

For a fleeting moment she wished she was a gossip, but that was like wishing she was petite, or beautiful, she chided herself, then wondered why she was anxious to know more! Gregor Ballantyne, past or present, was nothing more to her than the owner of the hospital in which she worked.

With a strong mental tug she shifted her thoughts back to the ward. Alexander Walsh had talked about business during her lunchtime visit, but an underlying anxiety in the man prompted her to go back in to see him before she went off duty.

'Who's next door?' was the man's greeting, as she walked quietly into his room.

'A Mrs Craig,' she told him.

'She'll drive you all mad before long,' he remarked. 'Her poor nurse is in and out of there all day! Doctors, too, by the look of things. At death's door, is she?'

'Not really,' Elly responded, grinning at her perceptive patient, 'and that's all I'm going to say. There are enough tales told out of school in this place as it is, without my adding to them.'

'Then stay and talk about other things,' he suggested. 'After all, a man's paying enough for this service. I could be in a five-star hotel for less!' Sensing again the fear his blustering was unable to conceal completely, she pulled up a chair.

'You know what they're doing to me tomorrow?'

She nodded. 'It's a fairly standard operation here. The surgeon will open up your carotid artery and scrape away the gunk that's collected on the walls from years of high living!'

'Hmph! Nice medical description that is, and you don't sound the least sympathetic!'

'Why waste my sympathy on a man who has brought this on himself with years of over-indulgence, and who, if he behaves himself and does exactly as he's told, will be out of here in three or four days.'

'That sounds like a threat whichever way I take it,' he grumbled.

'There are possibilities of complications after any operation,' she told him, 'and anything in the head or neck region is particularly delicate. I know Dr Blythe will have told you that already, but also pointed out that you'll be reducing the chance of a stroke enormously'.

'I thought the tablets I was taking were supposed to do that,' Alexander argued. 'I was started on Anturane, then switched to aspirin, and now the fellow reckons surgery is the only way to go.'

'That's because an angiogram must have detected signs of artherosclerotic plaque in the wall of your carotid artery. That's the gunk I told you about.'

She knew this would all have been explained to him before, but also knew how little patients took in when they were sitting in a doctor's surgery. Their presence in hospital usually forced them to consider the seriousness of their situation, and fear came creeping into their minds.

'The operation is simple enough, because, in your case, the occlusion is in the section of the artery outside your skull, and quite easy for the surgeon to reach.'

'Simple, huh? That fellow has already warned me of about ten things that can go wrong, ranging from blood clots in the neck that cut off my breathing, to nerve damage that might leave me a very different man.'

Elly smiled at him.

'He didn't mean to frighten you,' she said gently, recognising the source of his underlying unease. 'It's all part of giving the patient enough information to make what is now called 'an informed choice'. Doctors believe you should know what might happen before you opt for surgery, especially when it is only one form of treatment for a patient's condition.'

'There wasn't really a choice,' her patient grumbled, but he smiled as he spoke, and she reached out and patted his hand.

'If, when you recover from the operation, you choose to adopt a healthier lifestyle, you should live to a happy old age.'

'Never thought much about old age,' he admitted. 'At first it was too far off, and now the damn thing is too close.'

Elly was wondering what to reply to such a depressing statement, when Alison popped her head around the door-jamb.

'Dr Ballantyne would like to see you if you've got a minute, Sister.'

'I'd better go and see what he wants,' she said, with a rueful smile. 'There's not much time for quiet chats in a place this size! You'll have gone into Theatre before I come on duty in the morning, but I'll be thinking of you, and will be here when you get back to the ward.'

She patted his hand, and hurried out, wondering why this grouchy businessman should have wormed his way through her customary reserve.

Returning to the desk, she found that the hospital owner was wondering much the same thing.

'You seem to be spending an inordinate amount of time with a perfectly well patient, Sister Winthrop.'

Taken aback by this first salvo in a renewed bout of hostilities, she looked searchingly at his face, and was surprised to see his eyelids drop to hide something she could not understand in his grey eyes.

'I've increased Mrs Craig's medication slightly,' he went on to inform her in an elaborately precise tone. 'I've actually told her that it's been doubled, and I would appreciate it if you could ask the staff to go along with the notion.'

'Nurses don't discuss medication with patients,' she pointed out, swallowing an impulse to question the deception and protest at the need for it. 'They simply follow doctors' orders and point this out when questioned.'

He paused for a moment, as if taken aback by her caustic reply, then nodded and swung away down the corridor, his hands deep in his pockets, his shoulders slouched forward in a manner that somehow managed to imply both defensiveness and aggression.

Elly watched him with a peculiar regret seeping through her body like an elusive sadness.

Delighted hospital gossip about a male patient's pursuit of the redoubtable Sister Winthrop reached Gregor's ears three days later, and thudded into his body with a physical impact that made him wonder if he was sickening for something.

'Actually, behind all the sniggering, I think there are plenty of people on the staff who'd be pleased for Elly if something did come of it,' Sally Jeffs continued, as they sat over a morning coffee in his office. 'She's a very nice woman underneath that starchy exterior. I'm sure it's a protective front she puts up to prevent people from prying into her personal life—which isn't up to much.'

Sally's voice trailed off, as if she was thinking things she couldn't say—or regretting things she had said. Gregor found himself wanting to know more, but anything that faintly hinted of gossip was usually avoided at his regular meetings with Sally, and he didn't know how to prompt her without being blatantly obvious.

He detoured through Neurovascular a little later in day, using his patient as an excuse. Three vases of red roses adorned the desk, and must have multiplied, for there were more of them in every ward he looked into, even some in Room Fourteen.

'A new admirer?' he asked Jocee, nodding towards the bold brightness. He was rewarded by a flashing smile of malicious delight.

'Not mine, would you believe, darling,' she replied, 'but that thin red beanpole of a sister. It seems she's made a conquest and the man has been simply flooding the place with red roses since he regained consciousness.'

He'd forgotten his ex-wife's viperish tongue. She'd been so intent on her 'poor little me' act since she'd summoned him to Brisbane that he'd almost been taken in by her pathetic sweetness.

'It seems the patient next door is head over heels! Such a waste, you know! I believe he's practically king of the Gold Coast—indecently rich!—and here's poor little me on the look out for a man, and scars all over my face.'

She smiled beguilingly at him, but he was so sickened by the words that he could not react as he should, could not reassure her about her beauty, or maintain a pretence about the operation she had demanded from the Brisbane specialist although she was still in her thirties and her fine skin only faintly lined.

He realised she'd prevailed upon him to transfer her down here so her friends would not find out she was in hospital, and, worse still, come and visit her! She was also prolonging her departure, enjoying the attention until such time as her scars could be hidden under hair or skilfully applied make-up and she could emerge, more beautiful than ever, to face her artificial world. Suddenly, he was tired of the games Jocee played, and of his own weakness in continuing to indulge her.

The roses also annoyed him, out of place against the pale, pastel-coloured room, their scent heavy and cloying. And weren't red roses something of a cliché these days? They didn't suit the woman, anyway! He'd have chosen——

'I'll call in and see you tomorrow,' he said abruptly and strode out, praying the 'thin red beanpole' would not materialise in front of him when his temper had risen to boiling point. Again!

Elly, hovering in the pantry, watched him stalk past, an impression of some strongly suppressed feeling radiating from his body in invisible waves. Clive Evans had been right about his haunting the ward! Ex-wife she might be, but Jocee Craig, as she called herself, must still mean a great deal to him.

The realisation followed her home, and darkened her mood as she sat with her father, then performed the little rituals of the evening.

'You're lucky I'm an equable person,' she told Franny. 'A more feeling female would have kicked you by now. It's an established emotional outlet, kicking the cat!'

The blue eyes narrowed, and the phone shrilled, sounding abnormally loud in the quiet flat.

'Gregor Ballantyne here, Ellen,' the voice informed her, and Elly sank into the cane chair by the phone as a sick weakness spread through her body.

'I've been looking at a catamaran I might buy. It's a Hobie 16. I have sailed one by myself, but I'm out of practice and wondered if you'd be willing to come out with me.'

Was he offering out of kindness, because she'd said she must sail again? Or did he simply need a crew?

'I work weekends,' she told him, hoping her voice would not betray her agitation. She remembered that brief glimpse of his hands. Would he be able to handle the ropes on his own?

'I can make it Tuesday.'

Well, that's certainly blunt and to the point, she thought. No 'please', and certainly no false compliments about the pleasure of my company.

'I'd enjoy that.' She heard herself saying the words although she had no recollection of any conscious debate behind the decision.

'Good,' he replied. 'The fellow who's trying to sell it will rig it up, and I'll drop him off in front of your house about ten o'clock, providing there's some wind, of course.'

'At this time of the year, a howling southerly is almost inevitable. I presume you have a wetsuit, because you'll need it!' she informed him, hoping she sounded as curt and practical as he had when he'd issued his invitation.

But when he said goodbye and she heard the click that disconnected them, Elly crumpled down in the chair with a loud sigh, as if she'd been holding her breath since she first heard the sound of his voice.

A nervous restlessness shook her, and she wondered, for the first time, about her reactions to this man who had so disrupted her quiet existence. Could it be a physical attraction towards him that made her feel uncomfortable, and ill at ease in his presence?

She shook her head. One brief romance when she was a student had not provided much practical experience in matters of physical attraction, and her ensuing lack of interest in most members of the male species had led her to decide she was not a highly sexual being. Her life had a peaceful symmetry that pleased her, and she was inclined to blame any fleeting moments of dissatisfaction on a lack of mental stimulus, rather than the absence of a man from her life.

'Maybe I'm not one hundred per cent better after the concussion,' she excused herself to the cat. 'The queasiness I feel is a final remnant of the bang on the head.'

Her uncertainty was not helped when the man causing all her problems stopped by the desk next morning to speak to her about a minor procedural matter. There was no mention of the phone call or the forthcoming event. It was as if, having asked her, he had filed the subject away under Tuesday, and saw no need to refer to it again.

'I'm going off to one of those health farm places for a few weeks, in obedience to my doctor's orders. The fellow reckons I need to re-educate myself in sensible eating, but I'll be in touch with you, my girl,' Alexander Walsh announced very loudly, emerging from his room with his bag in his hand. Elly felt her face grow red as Gregor Ballantyne gave her a strange look and departed, and the members of her staff within hearing concealed grins, or turned away to stifle their laughter.

'Hardly a girl, Mr Walsh,' she responded drily, but she smiled at the magnate, knowing that underneath his showy, self-important exterior there was a clever, kind and amusing human being. His room had provided a refuge when Dr Ballantyne's frequent visits to Fourteen had disrupted her usual serenity, and the quiet conversations they'd enjoyed had added an extra dimension to her work. 'Take care of yourself,' she added, walking down the corridor towards the reception area with him.

'You too,' he replied, dropping his bag and planting a kiss on both her cheeks. Stunned by the gesture, she stood where she was, while he retrieved his belongings and strode off towards the front door.

'Admiring the carpet?'

The big figure didn't break stride as he hulked past her, throwing the remark at her as he stalked away, hands rammed into pockets, but his shoulders straighter today, giving her the impression of someone about to go into battle. She shuddered at the thought. As long as it wasn't against her this time!

She turned back towards the ward, and the work awaiting her there. Nothing changed! Yet everything was different, wasn't it? She shook her head. The new owner had certainly brought in some minor improvements, but nothing radical, nothing that would explain her feelings of dislocation.

The uneasiness remained, accelerating as her days off drew closer. It was characterised by a tightening of her stomach muscles whenever she caught a glimpse of Gregor Ballantyne in the corridor, and a burning tension in every muscle of her body when she didn't.

The wind had turned, and a fresh south-easter was flirting across the surface of the shimmering water as

Elly pulled a big shirt on over her short-sleeved, short-legged wetsuit. She saw the catamaran glide out from the beach beyond the marina as she spread sunscreen across her face and arms. Then the wind caught the sail and the skittish craft keeled up high, forcing the two men on board to fling themselves outwards to bring her back under control.

A flare of excitement scorched through Elly. It *was* too long since she had sailed. Slipping her feet into light rope-soled shoes, she caught up her beach bag and hurried downstairs, checking with Mrs Hobson that the carer they had arranged to sit with her father had arrived.

The white-hulled boat had been beached, and turned into the wind, by the time she crossed the road.

'Sailed one before?' the stranger asked, nodding approvingly at the leather mittens she was pulling on.

'Raced one,' she assured him, remembering the heady days when she and her father had competed regularly.

'Then you'll have no trouble,' he responded, and, with a wave to her boss who was opening the inspection hatch on one hull, he walked back towards the marina.

'Good morning,' Ellen said, carrying her waterproof bag towards the boat to stow by the mast. 'I brought some fruit and a bottle of mineral water, but if you want to stay out longer I could make some sandwiches.'

The words were stilted, stumbling awkwardly off her tongue. Mentally, she cursed the man for not being more forthcoming about his plans, while her stomach leapt about inside her body like a demented frog in a bottle.

'I brought some food,' he responded, his deep voice bearing its own hesitation as he waved to another bag secured to the mast. 'I thought we might picnic on the island.'

His eyes, which had moved swiftly over her as she approached, held hers, a strange, searching expression darkening their greyness. As her heartbeats accelerated to an erratic gallop, she looked quickly away, making an inane remark about the weather to cover her inner turmoil.

Maybe she was attracted to the man! If so, then her taste wasn't bad, she conceded, as she watched him screw the hatch cover back into place. His bare legs were tanned, the skin so taut over bone and muscle that he could have modelled for an anatomy lesson. Looking closer, she could see droplets of water caught in the dark hairs that covered the bunched muscles in his calves and her fingertips tingled with an urge to brush them away. He remained unaware of her scrutiny, so, with a rare trepidation, she continued to look and appraise, pleased by the flatness of his stomach and the swell of his biceps under the black rubber of his wetsuit.

'Ready?'

His voice brought her back to reality. Why should she be thankful that he was wearing a pair of baggy shorts over the wetsuit? the Sister Winthrop part of her mind demanded, but the Elly part only smiled weakly, and nodded at the man who was causing such tumult in her mind and body.

He handed her a buoyancy vest, and trapeze harness, and she shrugged out of her shirt and pushed it down into her bag, then concentrated on the fastenings of the vest and harness.

'If you'd hop on the trampoline and ready the jib sheet, I'll push her off and drop the rudders then handle the main.'

He spoke with a curt formality, although she was already climbing on to the trapeze, and for an instant she imagined him in an operating theatre, minimising his instructions into a few clipped orders. Then, all at once, she felt the surging lift as the hulls left the sand, and thoughts of work vanished as she fell into the rhythms she had learned as a teenager and they brought the skimming little craft about and beat up into the wind.

Her hair whipped around her face, and the exhilaration that only sailing could provide filled her with such joy that she could have cheered or laughed aloud. One hull lifted, kissing the water, and they swung out in counterbalance with a balletic symmetry and grace that matched the beauty of the craft.

He must have been serious about buying a cat, she realised, as she fought to keep in unison with him while he put the little craft through its various points of sailing, beating up through the channels, then running free before the wind.

'Had enough for the moment?' he yelled, as they came round Crab Island some hours later. She nodded. Much as she was enjoying it, she knew her arms were not used to the exercise, and she could feel her muscles beginning to tighten in a prelude to cramp.

'We'll free her off and reach into the beach there,' he suggested, pointing towards a shallowly shelving strip of sand on the foreshore of South Stradbroke.

The boat responded with a smooth surge of speed, sliding well up on to the sand with none of the jarring impatience of a roughly executed move. Satisfaction with the manoeuvre topped up the feeling of delight that had been growing in Elly since they first took off, and she slackened off the jib and leapt down on to the sand, flinging her arms into the air with a triumphant,

'Yeah, man!' and capering up and down like an idiot.

As the realisation of her company dawned on her, she turned with a shame-faced grin towards her fellow sailor, startling a peculiarly arrested kind of look on his face.

'It's a long time since I've sailed,' she muttered, embarrassed by her erratic behaviour.

'I'm glad you managed to enjoy it,' he said, the words devoid of any emotion, but a smile tugging at one corner of his mouth.

'Oh, I did,' she assured him, deciding it was useless to pretend indifference when the brief adventure had so obviously rejuvenated her spirits and released some unrecognised springs of tension in her body. 'She sails well, doesn't she?'

She patted one smooth hull, then looked up as he said, 'She does indeed,' with a suggestion of some hidden meaning behind the words.

'We've a hut here, if you'd like to wash some salt off and sit comfortably while we picnic,' she told him, and was pleased when he nodded.

Earlier in the day, she'd debated whether to tell him about the little holiday hut her family had owned for forty years, hidden away in the trees beyond the beach. Now it felt right, and somehow natural, so it was with a tingling sense of excitement that she helped drop the sails and secure the boat before picking up her bag and leading him across the sand to one of the many little tracks that led inland.

It was months since she'd visited the island, and years since she had brought anyone to this very special haven of peace and tranquillity, but she didn't question this man's place in her decision, merely leading him sure-footed through the dappled sunlight, beneath the wind-twisted branches of the foreshore scrub.

Gregor followed her in silence, bemused by the tricks of light and shade playing on her bright hair, and the slim shining whiteness of her bare legs. When he closed his eyes, he could see her dancing on the soft golden sand, some like wild free spirit delighting in the simple gift of life, and the rapture of living.

He focused back on to the black-clad shoulders, and the riotous red mass of damp, entangled hair, and desire sprang to life with a fierce, unnerving intensity.

The hut was just that, he realised, as they came into a sheltered clearing, overhung with she-oaks and misshapen banksia trees. It had once been painted green, he decided, but had faded to the drab colour of the surrounding bush, so it looked more like a part of nature than an intrusion of man into the landscape.

His guide had disappeared around the back of the building, and he stood and looked about with interest, while a sense of peace wrapped around him like a snug blanket. The air was warm, and redolent with the scent of a wattle, brazenly gold in the muted bush just beyond the house. Birds muttered in the trees, and the wind sighed softly, bringing its own benediction to the harmonious setting.

Then the front of the hut seemed to fold back on itself, as the woman who was having such a strange effect on him pushed open two wide doors, revealing a sparsely furnished but eminently practical interior.

Latching back the doors to let the winter sunshine flood in, she unfolded two deckchairs from the wall and set them up on the paved deck, then hitched a small wooden table forward with her foot before disappearing back inside to re-emerge with two glasses to put on it.

'I'm going to take my wetsuit off,' she announced, totally at ease in this, her own familiar setting. He watched her twist an arm behind her back and saw the grimace as stiff muscles protested at the motion.

'Here,' he said, moving swiftly to her side. 'Let me.'

She turned her back to him, like an obedient child, and, resting one hand on her shoulder to hold her steady, he slid the heavy corroded zip down, slowly and carefully, so the strands of fiery hair did not catch in the thick teeth.

As if feeling his distraction with her hair, she reached up, and her long, slim fingers grasped the waving mass and pulled it forward, so that the blackness of the wetsuit parted to reveal her skin, so pristine white, and fine and soft, that he held his breath.

Lower and lower the hard metal stub slid, past the narrow band of her black bikini top, to where her back curved away from him, and her waist slimmed in to a bare handspan before flaring out again to hint at the soft roundness of hips.

'I can manage now, I think,' she said softly, but she did not move away. He wondered if his sexual need had magnetised the air, holding her within the force-field of his libido.

'It is a long time,' he said judiciously, measuring each word with a careful amount of air so that they did not fail or falter, 'since I have felt like this.' His hand lifted off the zip, and reached up to settle on her other shoulder, slipping beneath the wetsuit to rest on the warmth of her skin. His fingers curled around the soft shape of their own accord, applying an even gentle pressure that he tried to prevent from being masterful or grasping.

'Even as a pubescent schoolboy I doubt I experienced such a blatant, agonising, inexplicable, outrageous desire for a woman as I feel for you now, Sister Winthrop,' he continued. 'I am telling you this before you realise it for yourself and wonder what kind of maniac you have brought to your retreat. I am also talking in the hope it will defuse some of the embarrassment I feel and maybe help me find a way through the confusion in my mind and the betrayal of my body.'

Still she did not move, but he could feel a tension in the flesh beneath his hand, and he stumbled over the words he hoped would reassure her.

'I'm not going to leap on you, or ask you to submit to my freakish desires,' he added, then spoiled his reassurances as words spilled out in a surrogate release, 'although the temptation to run my fingers down your back, to feel the silky softness of that white, white skin, is almost overwhelming. You have bewitched me, staid Sister Winthrop, with this other side of you that dances like a whirling dervish on the beach, then hides behind a shield of wild red hair. You lead me to this hidden glade on your enchanted island, and expect that I resist your provocation?'

Now he gave her a gentle push, but did not release her, drawing her back instead, to hold her lightly against his chest while he dropped one kiss on the whiteness that so mesmerised him.

'Celibate for too long,' he murmured, shame-faced and apologetic, and wondered, as she walked away from him into the dimness at the back of the hut, if he should take himself back down to the beach and swim for about an hour, or sell his hospital and go back to Melbourne, or just hope she'd put his behaviour down to a touch of the sun and handle it with the competent authority of the perfect, ice-cool, correct and punctilious ward sister he knew her to be!

Elly could feel the place where his lips had met her skin burning as fiercely as if he had pressed a burning brand against her back.

What did you say when a man you barely knew told you he was lusting after your body? After he had made love to you with velvet words that set your nerves on fire and made your body ache for some release it could not name? And how did you face him again and pretend nothing had happened?

Her thoughts tumbled over each other, jostling with the messages of want and need that her body was sending in rebellious waves, banishing common sense and practicality in a ferment of sexual longing that terrified her with its intensity. Had his words—his muttered, abject excuse of prolonged celibacy—awoken some unexplored demons of her own from a slumber deep beneath the calm surface of her life, or had his body sent its own silent messages, through her skin, and into her cells and blood and sinews.

As she peeled off the damp tight rubber she felt the awareness of her body, the tingling anticipation between her thighs, and the heavy, tautening fullness of her breasts. It was a betrayal that shocked her beyond belief. Her passive, obedient body responding like this to mere words, to an expression of what amounted to lechery, and the fleeting brush of a very chaste salute!

CHAPTER EIGHT

'LUNCHEON is served,' Gregor called as Elly ran a brush through her rebellious hair. Peering at her reflection in the age-spotted mirror, she decided she probably did look a pale shade of green, although she knew the mirror always did that to her skin.

She tugged at the big shirt, which was all the covering she'd brought with her, wishing it revealed a lot less leg.

You can handle this, she assured herself. You are intelligent, efficient, mature and capable. You *can* handle it!

He was already seated, facing away from her towards the bush, through which you could catch glimpses of sunlight on the water. On the small table between the chairs he had set out a big box of sandwiches, fresh, thick and crusty by the look of them.

Hunger forced her forward, and she dropped into the vacant chair, intending only to eat and leave the conversation to him.

He had stripped off his wetsuit and was wearing the baggy shorts and a faded cotton shirt, and he looked comfortable and at ease, as natural and at home as he was in his three-piece suit striding through the hospital corridors. Like a chameleon, he fitted into whatever environment he happened to enter, and it told her of a confidence in the man that she had to envy.

Shrugging off the undermining unease, she turned towards him with a tentative grin and a feeble comment about the difficulty of cutting fresh bread straight.

'You are a remarkable woman,' was all he said, but the smile that accompanied the words was very peculiar. It was kind, but somehow twisted, as if the effort was hurting him somewhere deep inside. She knew that, because it hurt her as well, although she didn't for one minute believe that hearts could ache.

'I am sorry for embarrassing you with my meanderings,' he added, the quiet words delivered with care, although his eyes were fixed, unseeing, on the scene in front of them. 'I seem to react in an extraordinary way when I am with you, although you are not the kind of woman I. . .'

The words died away, and the soft sounds of the bush faded momentarily with them, leaving a silence that had its own comfort.

'Usually take for a lover?' Elly suggested, half mocking but still anxious that the conversation continue. It might help untangle her own confusion.

His head swung around, and once again she saw that startled expression in his eyes. This time the smile was rueful, and he nodded.

'There've not been that many,' he protested. 'I married young, then, when that broke up, I played around a bit, but I found it wasn't a game I fancied——'

'Although you were good at it,' Elly interjected, as much to see him smile as to pry out the extra information.

She was rewarded with the smile, and a quick nod.

'But the women I played with knew the rules, Elly.' The use of her name sent tremors down her spine. 'They played it all the time and knew it was just a game!'

'And I don't!' she said flatly, as the sandwich she was chewing became dry and tasteless in her mouth. There was an awkward pause, and she could have kicked herself for causing it. Better to have kept her mouth shut and let him ramble on, she decided moodily, but it was too late now.

'You might,' he commented at last, 'but. . .'

'I don't seem that kind of girl,' she finished for him, bitterness adding a bite as sharp as mustard to the words.

'I wasn't going to say that,' he demurred, but his tone lacked conviction, and she forced away an overwhelming regret for all the things she wasn't—like pretty, and flirtatious, and evenly tanned, and brunette!

'It's true, anyway,' she told him evenly. 'I'm not that kind of girl. I don't think I'm embittered, but I'm definitely spinsterish—complete with cat! My life is ordered and——' until recently, she thought, but did not say '—very satisfying.'

'Even though you're nursing when your heart is in research?'

The percipience of his remark shocked her out of the mood of mild self-pity, and she turned to look at him, growing uncomfortably warm when she saw the smile in his deep-set eyes.

'You couldn't hide your enthusiasm when you started talking about the trials,' he explained. 'It didn't take much brain power to work out where your first interests lie. Did you think about further study, or have you only recently realised that you have an ability in the area of research? The conciseness of your work is surely proof of that!'

The switch back to rational conversation pleased her, and the tension she hadn't realised was still present, slid out of her body.

'I had started postgraduate study, before I decided to shift down here.' That was the truth, and, suddenly, it was all she wanted to say. Maybe the conversational switch wasn't quite as providential as she'd hoped!

'For your father's sake?'

She looked away towards the trees, and nodded.

'My mother died when I was six. My father brought me up. He was a clever man, and must have had many offers to lecture overseas, to be on committees and chair conferences, but he was always there for me, not in any self-sacrificing way, but because, it seemed to me, he wanted to be there.'

'It was his choice,' her companion said quietly, and she sighed.

'It was, but done so quietly I didn't realise until I started nursing and learned of his standing in the medical world that it would have been a sacrifice on his part; that there would have been many opportunities he let pass by.'

'So now you're making your own sacrifice!' The words were quietly spoken but she fancied she heard a touch of contempt behind them, and was quick to refute his claims.

'It has nothing to do with sacrifice,' she assured him, her chin tilting so she could glare into his eyes and emphasise her point. 'Once I realised that the man I loved was slipping away, I wanted to spend as much time as I could with him. There was no choice.'

'So you left one road and took another, and don't feel bitterness or regret. Will you have me believe you're such a paragon, Sister Winthrop?'

His eyes held a query that wasn't quite as light as the words, and she tried to answer honestly. 'I feel frustrated at times,' she admitted. 'Now and then, it seems as if my life is on hold. I suppose I envy people like yourself, who are free to take a new direction while I am tied up at a crossroads.'

'And I envy you your acceptance of your fate,' he said, and reached across the space between them and took her hand. 'Is there a beach side of your island we can walk to?' he asked, rising to his feet as if the inactivity was somehow irking him.

She let him pull her up, then slipped her hand out of his and led him around the hut to a worn track.

'I was forced into a new direction,' he said, falling in behind her on the narrow track. 'Forced, kicking and screaming, and railing against the fates.'

'I saw your hands,' she murmured, looking back over her shoulder to see him following, head lowered, and hands, as usual, hidden in his pockets.

'Arthritis, of all things!' he told her savagely. 'It doesn't even run in the family!'

'Couldn't you have remained in practice, as a consultant, and continued your research?'

She could almost hear the change in his mood in the slowing shuffle of his feet on the sandy path, and the soft sighing sound as he released his pent-up breath.

'I suppose I could have,' he admitted, 'but at the time I was so angry, so devastated, that all I wanted was to get out. If I couldn't operate, then I didn't want to be a doctor—to me it was as simple as that. I saw the advertisement for the sale of the hospital in a national paper, and began negotiations immediately.'

'Thinking it would fulfil a need?'

'Thinking I'd become a businessman and make a lot of money—start a chain of hospitals perhaps!'

'Fast food's an easier business,' she suggested, and was pleased to hear him chuckle.

'Yes, the hospital was a mistake,' he told her. 'I imagined, because I knew something about hospitals, that it would make the ideal business venture, but it hasn't worked out that way. It's underlined all that I've lost.'

He sounded so *distrait* she stopped, and turned around, so that his next step brought him to within inches of her body. Looking up into his eyes, she raised her hands and rested them on his shoulders.

'With your knowledge and experience, you can add an extra dimension to the hospital, but you don't have to torture yourself by being there all the time. If you don't want to practise, why not teach? Impart some of your knowledge to the next generation, and instil in them a desire to keep searching.'

Was she getting through to him, or was he writing off her words as more of the dreaded 'Pollyanna-isms' he'd accused her of once before? Then, as she wondered, his head moved lower, and his lips met hers in a gentle, tender kiss, not sexual at all, but tinged with the sadness of infinite regret.

Then he lifted his head and looked down into her eyes with an unreadable expression on his face.

'You are a very lovely lady, Elly Winthrop,' he said at last. 'Now, where's your beach?'

The time for true confessions was over, she realised, and turned away to lead him up and over the first of the three long sand dunes that protected the island from the encroaching might of the ocean.

'I wouldn't have believed it possible that this great deserted stretch of sand could co-exist so closely with the over-populated beaches of the Gold Coast,' he remarked, nodding to where the high-rise buildings of that city blotted out the southern horizon. 'I'd like to spend more time here, but I guess we'd better get back to the boat. The poor guy will think I've stolen it.'

He was all calm, cool practicality! She might have dreamt the fervour of his words, and imagined the fleeting touch of burning lips. She should be pleased, she told herself as they turned and walked back towards the hut. He was quite right! She wasn't the kind of woman who indulged in light-hearted affairs, was she?

The thoughts scudded across her mind like storm clouds blown by unpredictable winds, and, while part of her intelligent self admitted that she probably could not handle an affair with this man, another part felt cheated. It would have been nice to have been asked, she decided, with a stubbornly lingering sense of regret.

'I'll drop you on the beach and take the boat back to its owner under the mainsail,' he yelled against the wind as they whipped back across the Broadwater a little later.

Which ends any chance of your inviting him in for coffee, or pushing this questionable 'friendship' any further than he wants it to go, Elly realised. She helped him lower the jib and stow it, then watched him race the little craft away, her hand raised in farewell, before walking up the strip of sand towards a home that she knew would seem lonely and uninviting.

The noise that woke her next morning sounded exactly like pebbles being thrown against glass, and merged into a dream she was having, so that, when she heard it again, she shook her head in disbelief.

It was still dark in her bedroom, but the sky was lightening outside the veranda windows. Across the water, the first vestiges of colour from the rising sun were touching the low bank of clouds above the island. About six, she decided, then saw the rain of tiny stones hit the glass and slide back out of sight.

Leaping out of bed, she rushed across to push open

the window and peer uncertainly into the gloom. His shape and size were unmistakable, and he stood beneath her, his arms outstretched, as if in resignation.

'Could I talk to you for just a minute?' he hissed, but she was too bemused to answer.

As her head disappeared from view, Gregor wrapped his arms around his body and tried to still the trembling that had been growing steadily since two o'clock, when he'd at last decided sleep was impossible, and had found a possible solution to his problem. So much depended on her now!

The front door was opening silently, and he crossed the yard and hurried in, immediately aware of the warmth of the woman he desired so irrationally, and the musky, sexy smell of sleepy femininity.

'I'm sorry——' he stammered, but she cut him off with a swift hand to his lips, then led him up the stairs to her own domain.

'I had to see you or go crazy,' he told her when she turned to face him in the big dim room. 'In fact, I've probably gone crazy—look,' he said, and held out a hand that shook as if with fever.

She stood so silently that he wondered if he could say the words he'd practised. Behind her, the sky was going mad with colour, but the strengthening light outside cast her face into shadow, so it was impossible to read her thoughts. The reflected glow touched her tousled hair, turning it to a burnished bush of flaming red, and, beneath its weight, her slim shape seemed almost fragile in the pale green silky nightdress she was wearing.

'I've come——' he started again, but then found the words impossible to say.

Elly watched him, afraid to move lest she break some spell she couldn't comprehend, but felt as strongly as a physical force. The silence plucked at her nerves, until she wanted to cry out, but she forced herself to exert the control that was an essential part of her maturity.

'Would you like a cup of tea or coffee?' she whispered, in a voice that was as uncertain as his hand.

'Not yet,' he said crossly, as if it was her fault he was standing shaking in her living-room at six-thirty in the morning. 'I want to ask you something!'

'Ask away,' she said with a false gaiety that covered a monumental panic. He was going to ask her to go to bed with him! Going to suggest an affair! What would she say? Why hadn't she thought about this? Rehearsed their parts in the mad charade and decided what she could say if it happened? Because you didn't think he'd ask, she reminded herself. In fact, you imagined you were sorry he didn't!

'Will you marry me?'

Her mind was so busy chasing her own questions and answers that the query, posed at last, in a gruff, strangled croak, made no sense to her at all.

'I think we'd better have coffee,' she said in her best no-nonsense ward sister voice, and, reaching out a hand, she took a firm grip on his muscled forearm, and led him towards the veranda. 'Sit there while I fix it,' she ordered, then hurried off to the kitchen, where she clung to the benchtop and shook for a little while herself.

He must be mad, she decided finally, setting plates, cups and saucers on a tray while the water boiled and some bread toasted.

'Will you?' he asked, his voice deeper now, and almost desperate, as she unloaded the tray on to a low table between the chairs.

She shook her head and went back into the kitchen, returning with coffee and toast, and pouring him a cup before she sat down herself.

'Marriage is a fairly drastic way of satisfying lust, isn't it?' she said as lightly as she could. 'I gathered affairs were more your style.'

She studied him intently as she spoke, and could see that the trembling was easing, and the hand that lifted the coffee-cup to his lips barely shook at all. Following the movement, she saw the greyness in his face, accentuated by the new shininess of his skin where he'd scraped a razor over his beard before coming to see her.

'I thought we'd already established that you weren't that kind of woman,' he said, his voice rasping harshly as if the words were causing an obstruction in his throat.

'So you'd marry me? That's ridiculous!' She heard the stridency in her voice, but had to continue. 'We don't know each other.'

He looked up at her, and the sun caught his face, dispelling the greyness, and adding a warmth that the sudden sweet smile only served to emphasise.

'I know it's crazy,' he said. 'I've been telling myself that for the last four hours, but it seems like the only answer.'

His gaze had not left her face while he spoke, and the steady regard distracted her. It was as if his eyes were saying things his lips could not, but she was unable to read the message in them. She was confused, and a little afraid, yet, at the same time, her body was responding to his presence with an increasingly urgent hunger.

'Let's just have an affair,' she muttered, annoyed with him for opening a door to a secret room that promised a plethora of delights, and with herself for responding to him and being tempted to enter it. 'But only on condition that there's no one else in your life at the moment who'll be hurt by it, and that it is kept between the two of us.'

'That's a joyous response to a proposal of marriage,' he replied, with a dour grimace. 'Let's have an affair instead, she says! And why the secrecy proviso? Is it that you're ashamed to be seen with me, or afraid that it might make you appear human?'

She flinched under the whip of anger in his voice, but held her ground. Although it might not have been her first choice, the career she had forged for herself at Gracemere was important to her, and her work would continue to provide satisfaction long after Gregor Ballantyne had left the scene.

'I need to work,' she told him quietly, 'and the hours and position at Gracemere are ideal for me.' She paused, looking at him, to see if there might be a glimmer of understanding in his eyes, but his head was turned away, towards the stretch of water now taking colour from a rising sun. 'It would be untenable for me to continue there if it became known, particularly—' she swallowed a lump that had grown in her throat, and drew a deep, steadying breath '—after it had finished.'

'You're assuming it will?' There was no understanding in the abrupt question.

'Aren't you?' she countered.

'I wouldn't have offered marriage if I thought that,' he stated calmly, but she sensed the uncertainty behind the argument.

'But we don't know each other,' she bleated again. 'The whole thing's irrational.'

'Even the affair, Elly?' he asked, reaching out to

touch her arm, the hoarseness of despair back in his voice.

His fingers were as hot as fire on her skin, as if a fever burnt beneath the well-tended hand. Made breathless by this lightest of contacts, she studied the hand, as if to divine some answer from its long slim fingers, with the slightly swollen joints, and pale, close-cut nails.

Then the hand clenched against her arm and she heard a muttered curse from the man who had thrown her world into such chaos.

'There is no one else in my life at present, no romantic interest, no one who would be hurt,' he said in a stony voice. 'I promise to be as circumspect as you like, and not force my presence on you at inconvenient times, but I want you so badly, Elly, I can think of nothing else. If an affair is best for you, then I'll go along with that.'

Did he sound relieved? she wondered, then the reality of what he had said struck her and a thick soupy fog of doubt and shock and tremulous desire blotted out all thought processes.

The sun shone through the windows, warming her skin, and downstairs she could hear the Hobsons moving into the routine of their day, but she sat unmoving, like a detached jumble of bones and flesh.

'Changed your mind?' he asked, his voice so soft and gentle that it cut through the cloud that enveloped her, and she looked across to see him smiling again.

He was beyond her ken, this man who changed from stern to soft so rapidly that she had trouble keeping up.

She pushed away an urgent impulse to run and hide in a dark cupboard. Knowing he was experienced enough to read her embarrassment whatever she said or did, she looked directly into his eyes and shrugged.

'I don't know what to do next,' she said.

Gregor felt a physical shock of success—if it was success—jolt through his bones. Yet, now she was so nearly his, he wanted only to go to her and hold her; to lift her on his knee and soothe away the fear and consternation he could read in her eyes and see in the straining tension of her body. Wanted to tell her it didn't matter, that he was sorry he'd upset her with his dreadful declarations and sudden, stupid, frightening proposal; but his body was still held in thrall, and, more than all of this, he wanted to possess her.

'We could go to bed,' he said, marvelling at the fact that his voice came out at all, considering the difficulty he was having with his breathing. 'That is if it's convenient for you, and not going to upset your household.'

He sounded so humble she wanted to laugh, but her insides were trembling with such violence she was certain it would come out all wrong. How could they be sitting on her veranda at seven o'clock in the morning, discussing sin and seduction in such a forthright manner? It was crazy!

And as for my household? she thought, What do I do? Call out and tell Mrs Hobson that I won't be down to see my father because there's a man who wants to go to bed with me! Or leave the announcement till later when he's leaving for work, or whatever it is he intends doing the rest of the day.

Tears of despair and frustration began to gather in her eyes, and she shook her head, realising that it was never going to work. She had called his bluff, and now he'd accepted her challenge, he expected her to know what to do next—to organise things—to arrange the practical side of it as if she'd done it a dozen times before!

His hand slipped along her arm to grasp her fingers, and he pulled her up out of the chair and drew her close against his chest.

'Or we could start with a kiss now, and think about the rest a little later,' he murmured into her hair. 'Marriage might have been simpler, but we'll work around the problems, if an affair is all you want.'

The words had a tenderness that made her ache all over, and she slid her arms around his neck and clung to him.

'Do you usually spend your days off with your father?' he asked, and she nodded against his chest.

'And because you were out for the day yesterday, today is set aside for him?'

Again she nodded.

'That's OK, Elly,' he said, and his voice was a caress. 'I can wait—although I don't know for how long.'

His body moved against hers and she felt his hardness, then shuddered as her body echoed his need.

'I can arrange someone to care for my father and we could go to the island on my next days off,' she mumbled, and his arms tightened around her.

'Maybe it's a good thing I've got a trip to Melbourne planned for this week,' he said, dropping his head so that his lips moved against the skin at the nape of her neck, sending tremors of desire flickering through her veins. 'I might have found it difficult to stick to the "hands off" policy at work.'

The thought of his going away made her arms tighten involuntarily round his neck, as if to keep him physically close to her.

'When do you go?' she asked, pleased that her voice sounded quite normal in the midst of all this madness.

'This afternoon!' he said, and pushed her away, effectively stopping all conversation with a kiss that stole the breath from her parted lips, and promised such sweet rapture that she wanted it to last forever. 'I should be back at the hotel getting packed right now, but I couldn't leave without seeing you and talking to you and finding out if you felt anything at all towards me.'

His lips claimed hers again, seeming to drink the very essence of her soul in long, demanding draughts.

'You do, don't you?' he murmured against the softness. 'You do feel this—this *whatever* that seems to be pulling us together.'

Elly's heart fluttered indecisively in her chest, but the doubt behind his words gave her a strange confidence in herself, and an awakening power she had not realised she might possess. Tread lightly, Elly, an inner voice warned, but a little of the happiness she was beginning to experience could not be contained.

' "This whatever", Dr Ballantyne?' she repeated incredulously, teasing his lips with the tip of her tongue as she drew out the words. 'Is that a rational scientific explanation?'

He groaned and pulled her closer, his arms wrapping around her so tightly that she could barely breathe.

'I haven't had a rational idea for days,' he replied. 'If you only knew how long it took me to work out the boat idea, then the machinations I had to follow to find one I could borrow for the day. . .'

She heard the words, but they barely registered, as his lips were tracing a path across her skin, down her neck towards the base of her throat, lingering, pressing, moving on, electrifying the nerves so that her whole body was alight with tiny pinpricks of sensation and her knees went weak with the urgency of her desire.

'I've got to go and pack,' he said, but she no longer

had the strength to remove her arms from round his neck, nor any certainty that her legs would support her if she let go.

Tread lightly, Elly, the inner voice repeated, and she forced herself to push away from him, and tried to stem the flow of blood she could feel mounting to her cheeks as she realised what she must look like.

Brilliant timing, Ballantyne! Gregor thought as he felt the aching emptiness of his arms and the cold sensation in his skin when her body withdrew its warmth. Five days in Melbourne! Five days for her to change her mind—or come to her senses, more like!

He watched her push at the mass of hair, and saw the realisation of her state of undress and the quick shame quite clearly in her eyes, and again he cursed himself for his ineptitude in this bizarre courtship.

'If Mrs Hobson's about, I'll tell her I had to see you about something at the hospital, and couldn't leave it till later because of the Melbourne trip.' He watched her anxiously as he spoke, hoping to see her face relax and the embarrassment die out of her eyes.

'There's no need for that,' she said quietly, the greenness turning on him, as clear as the water beyond the windows. 'I'll tell Mrs Hobson one day soon. She's an incurable romantic and will be delighted for me.'

Although her eyes held his and her voice was steady, he detected a tautness in her composure that would crack quite easily, and again he wondered how he could disrupt her life this way, to satisfy what was probably just a normal carnal urge.

Or was it? he wondered, kissing her cheek and hurrying away from her distracting presence. If that was all it was, why did he care how she felt? Why was he so worried she might get hurt? Why had he offered to marry her?

He nodded absentmindedly to Mrs Hobson, who was sweeping the entry foyer, and walked out into the bright winter sunshine, refusing to look up at the window, lest he see her and have to go back in, to kiss her one last time, and hold her slim body to his for just a moment longer.

CHAPTER NINE

ELLY began to wonder about schizophrenia as she found herself functioning on two levels. Her body and what was needed of her mind performed the routine tasks that got her safely through the day with what she hoped was a semblance of normality, but another Elly walked beside her, filled alternately with excitement and doubt.

The weird duality accompanied her back to work, where vases of fresh red roses suggested that Alexander Walsh had placed a standing order at the local florist. Or? Her heartbeats quickened as she searched for a card, then fluttered almost to a halt when she read the note from Alexander.

She would ring the florist and tell them not to send any more, she decided, then promptly forgot about them when confronted with the problems of the day.

'Mrs Craig has left us! I know you'll be sorry to hear that!' the shift sister told her with a wide grin. 'And Kathryn's been discharged as well, but don't think you're in for a lazy day—there are seven new admissions and two accident victims expected in from Intensive Care. There's also a linear skull fracture in Seventeen, who should have been in Intensive Care, but they were full. Jenny Grimes, who worked in Intensive Care at one stage, is specialling him, but the younger staff are all upset because most of them know the lad—local heart-throb from what I can gather.'

Elly felt her normal self click into gear, absorbing all the information she was hearing and reading, her mind already allotting tasks and planning out the day.

'Good morning, Sister!'

Debbie's cheerful greeting brought the second Elly charging into her mind, and, without a thought for the consequences she blurted out the question that had nagged at the back of her subconscious for twenty-four hours.

'Why did you not want to nurse Mrs Craig?'

'Because she's Gregor's—that is, Dr Ballantyne's—ex-wife,' the young woman replied ingenuously.

Elly waited for more, a queer sick feeling in the pit of her stomach.

The more, when it came, slowly and hesitantly, as if Debbie was weighing each word, hurt her more than she expected, but in a different way.

'She hurt Gregor very badly, so much that Mum says he'll never be the same again—never really be free of her and happy in. . .' Debbie's face screwed up as she searched for the word she needed to explain. 'In an uncomplicated kind of way. Mum says he built a big wall around himself, that just got higher when he discovered he couldn't operate any more.'

And who is 'Mum' that she's such an authority? Elly longed to ask, but she sensed Debbie's withdrawal, and knew that to ask any more would be prying.

'I see you're down for Seventeen,' she said instead, switching back to work matters with an almost visible effort. 'Are you handling it all right?'

Debbie nodded. 'Jenny knows exactly what to do for him, and I just help her, and relieve her when she needs a break.'

'And your preceptor?' Elly asked, not having seen the older woman come in.

'She's off sick again. It seems she came back too soon after the flu, and has another dose, but all the nurses are helping me, and I have learned to move faster and get all my work done in the eight hours.'

Elly smiled at the earnest statement, then turned to greet Clive Evans.

'Young Stewart Crosby in Seventeen is mine,' he said, leading her towards the single room. 'Silly young fool came off a skateboard of all things—pinched his little brother's and was showing off to aggravate the kid, and came down on the edge of the gutter. We're monitoring IV input including medications against urinary output, and I've got the lab watching for abnormalities in electrolytes and arterial blood gases.'

'You're happy with Jenny Grimes?'

'Asked for her specially. She's a fine nurse and knows what to look for, is a dab hand at turning comatose patients, and seems to have a sixth sense about danger signals.'

'Who's doing nights?' Elly asked, knowing the supply of 'specials' was limited.

'A friend of Jenny's who trained in the public hospital, and has specialised in Intensive Care. She's good.'

Elly nodded, and they entered Room Seventeen together, smiling at the nurse who sat by the bed of the young man. The elevated head of the bed made it look as if he was leaning up to greet them, but the immobilised face showed no sign of awareness.

He was a good-looking young man with the tanned skin and sunbleached hair of a surfer, and Elly knew the physical fitness that still shone from his skin would help him in his fight towards a full recovery.

Clive finished reading the notes and handed them to Elly while he motioned to Jenny to follow him outside. Recent studies suggested a consistent rise in intra-cranial pressure in coma patients when conversations were carried on beside their beds, and the hospital had instituted strict procedures to follow in all cases.

After reading the notes, Elly waited for Jenny to return, then joined Clive outside the door, and listened to his instructions.

'I've inserted an intraventricular catheter for CSF drainage. It should help prevent rises in intracranial pressure, but I'd still like him kept as calm as possible. He needs to be suctioned to prevent respiratory insufficiency, but make sure if anyone but the "special" does it, it should be of no more than fifteen seconds' duration. It increases agitation and that increases pressure.'

Elly nodded. Whatever they could do to prevent a rise in intracranial pressure would make the lad's chances of a full recovery so much greater.

'Then there's the IV therapy. Although mild fluid restriction is desirable, you know the risk we run with dehydration.'

Clive's concern for the boy was underlined by the repetition of instructions, and Elly felt a sudden spurt of sympathy for him, knowing how useless he must feel, and how anxious he must be about the eventual outcome. The chances of permanent brain damage increased with every variation in the delicate balance of cerebrospinal fluid, of oxygen in the blood, of blood-pressure, and changes in temperature. It was the kind of monitoring that Intensive Care normally undertook, because they had the necessary devices, and staff, but it had been done on wards long before IC units had existed, and, in many hospitals, was still part of normal nursing duties.

'You're using isotonic fluids intravenously,' she said soothingly. 'As long as we monitor fluids in and out, we should be able to keep him just slightly euvolemic.'

'But it's a lot of extra responsibility to put on you

and the "specials", the constant monitoring and the regular blood and urine sampling for the lab.'

'We can do it,' Elly assured him with a smile.

'I'll be back this afternoon but call me if there's any change,' he ordered as he departed, and she realised that it was his manner, not his skill level or dedication, that irritated her.

She walked back to the desk, greeting Grant with a warm smile

'Two more carotid endarterectomies coming in this afternoon. I do hope you don't have the same effect on them as you did on Alexander,' Grant joked.

Elly slid a strained smile into place. Alexander Walsh was not making any secret of his attraction, and for a moment she wondered whether to be glad of it, simply because it would divert any possible attention away from herself and Gregor. Then she felt a flush of shame, that she would sink so low as to think of using someone's genuine regard in such a way!

'I think it highly unlikely,' she said crisply to Grant, nodding to two other specialists who were waiting by the desk. It was her last non-medical thought of the day, which progressed from normal chaos to pandemonium, as trivial incidents erupted with such frequency that she wondered if the fates had turned against her.

'Phone, Elly!'

She debated whether to take the call. She should have been off duty two hours earlier, but tying up loose ends from the new admissions had kept her anchored to the place.

'When you weren't at home, I figured you'd still be working, then I started panicking about you walking out into the car park on your own, and I broke your rules immediately.'

Gregor's voice, muffled by the self-deprecating grin she could picture on his face, reached across the miles and touched her heart.

'Are you there?' he asked, and she nodded, then realised that wasn't doing any good.

'I'm here,' she murmured, and prayed that no one was watching her, as her mind registered that her body was shaking all over.

'Here's my number,' he said, crisply now, as if it was purely business. 'Ring me when you get home, or a little later than that, so I can at least eat my dinner without worrying.'

She picked up a pen and jotted down the numbers, noting the irregularity of her writing with a clinical detachment.

'Elly, I. . .'

She waited, alerted by a sudden change in the tone of his voice, and a barely perceptible tremor.

'There are songs about this kind of thing, Sister Winthrop,' he said into the silence she couldn't break. 'But I've never believed them before.'

And with a click he was gone, the buzzing of the disconnected line reminding her of the automatic switchboard in the front office. The phone was safe from eavesdroppers, but how transparent was her face? Was the juvenile thrill that still ricocheted through her visible for all to see?

She picked up Alexander's roses, vase and all, deciding to take them home for Mrs Hobson, and floated down the corridor towards the car park. She couldn't possibly be in love! Love was for adolescents, not old maids of twenty-eight. What was more, he only wanted an affair! Or was it she who only wanted an affair? He only wanted her body—and that was the weirdest of all! It wasn't a body men usually lusted after. Her mind flirted with chemistry. What was the word in use so frequently of late? Pheromones!

'Phone again!' The voice was following her and she turned around, and saw the sister beckoning wildly. He wouldn't have rung again, unless he'd decided to say whatever it was he'd started earlier!

Her mind was so full of Gregor that it took a few seconds to realise what Mrs Hobson was telling her.

'I told the ambulance to take him to Accident and Emergency at Gracemere. I knew that would be what you wanted. It happened so suddenly, Elly. One minute he was on his feet and the next minute on the floor. His head must have struck that small table by his bed.'

Beyond the shock she heard the tears in the woman's voice, and she murmured soothing, meaningless phrases to reassure her that there was no question of blame in her mind.

'I'll call you after the doctor has seen him,' she told Mrs Hobson, then walked towards the wing where her father would be admitted.

He was unconscious, Mrs Hobson had said. Would concussion accelerate the deterioration? she wondered, then was shocked by her clinical reaction.

'The ambulance phoned through and we've called Clive Evans,' the doctor on duty at A and E informed her. At that moment the ambulance pulled in and she watched the staff move automatically through their paces, and saw the pale, motionless old man who'd been her father wheeled past her towards the first of the emergency care rooms.

She waited where she was, knowing how busy the staff would be and accepting that she would only be in the way. In her mind, she followed all the stages, seeing one nurse jotting down pulse and blood-pressure while another tried to raise a vein in his emaciated old arm to insert a needle for a drip.

Once they had him stabilised, it would be down to X-ray, then back up for Clive to examine, and add his expertise to the efficient team at present doing all they could.

Did she want him to die?

That she could think such a thing shocked her immeasurably and she shook with a sudden coldness that seemed to emanate from the marrow of her bones.

But if there was further brain damage, could she sit here praying that he would live?

Her mind blanked out, and she sat and shivered, unaware of the figures who flitted around her, of the sympathetic glances of her colleagues, and the hushed offers of tea and coffee.

'We can't do much more than make him comfortable,' Clive was saying, squeezing her cold hand as if trying to press the words through her skin. 'He has struck his head just above the temple; there's a fracture there, probably because his bone density would be low. I'm inclined to think he may have had a stroke which caused the fall, Elly. There's no response to stimuli.'

The words ceased for a moment, and she realised Clive was waiting for her to respond in some way, but her mind refused to work. Eventually, Clive continued, telling her things as if they had happened to someone else, a patient in her ward, not her father.

'His blood-pressure is elevated but his pulse is slow; his pupils also suggest some intracranial bleeding, but if we do a scan and find where it is he's unlikely to survive an operation to release the pressure, and with some degree of atrophy already present in the brain. . .'

She sat on, her mind finishing the sentence, knowing

they did not intervene in such cases, yet not knowing what to say, unable to decide what Clive expected of her.

'He's dying, Elly,' he added, forcing the words on her as if that would make the fact more believable. 'Do you want to sit with him?'

She nodded, understanding now, and, suddenly, unbearably, overwhelmed with sadness that she knew she should not feel.

With a gentleness she did not recognise, Clive led her into the little room, and pushed her into a chair. She reached out and took her father's hand, seeing the shape of bone and tendon beneath the transparency of his skin, and feeling the faint, fitful beats of his heart, like the ragged ticks of an unwound clock running down.

Then she looked at his face, and the snow-white hair; and remembered him yelling joyously into the wind as they raced across the Broadwater in their little skiff; saw that same hair plastered against his skull, as they battled the wind and rain to walk across the island and see the terrible fury of the ocean, whipped up by the tail end of a cyclone.

How they had laughed as they pitted themselves against the elements, how he had enjoyed his fights against the unknown in his research!

She smiled at him now, and nodded. The massive intellect that had been his would no longer be trapped in a brain that refused to work properly, and the indignity of the final years of his life would at last be ended.

And, while she could never have wished for him to die in order to obtain this release, she was resigned now that the time had come, and could be glad for him.

This time, when someone offered coffee, she accepted it, and asked the nurse who brought it in to

ring Mrs Hobson and let her know what was happening.

'Would you ask her to phone my brothers, and tell
her I could be very late?' she added, then wondered
if there wasn't something else she meant to do!

It was three o'clock in the morning before she finally
left, having had to take care of all the official details
of death. She trudged back to the main hospital to
reach the corridor that led down into the staff car
park. The familiarity of the building soothed her, and
tiredness brought its own anaesthesia.

There was a sense of unreality in the sight of the
young man jogging towards her, anxiety—or was it
fear?—in every line of his body. Someone he knew in
danger? Someone he must see before it was too late?
She was too tired to think about him, and turned her
head away as he was about to pass so he would not
see the stains of tears on her face.

The movement left her off balance when his arm
snaked round her neck, something hard pressed against
her backbone and he pushed her roughly back the way
she had come, but not towards the populated world
of A and E, but down the dimmer passage towards
the wards—her ward!

'I don't want to hurt you,' he panted into her ear,
his breath hot and fetid with the odour of bad teeth.
'Just give me some pethidine, morphine, whatever
you've got, and I'll disappear. No one need ever know.'

'People will notice if you're pushing me along like this,
and I'm off duty. I haven't a key. If you join the drug
rehabilitation programme you can get some supplies
legally, you know.' She babbled at him although she
told herself to speak calmly, and the unlikelihood of
being a victim again within a place she had regarded
as safe added to the unreality of the situation.

Part of her brain registered that she should be afraid, but there was no fear hovering at the edges of her mind, although she did feel an urge to laugh, which she put down to the beginnings of hysteria. How could you laugh when your father had just died?

With a kind of dazed common sense she tried to persuade the young man to take her to the interview-room. The corridor was empty in front of them but any moment now a night-duty nurse could appear and could start to panic. Was it actually a gun he had pressed against her back?

'Oh, Elly, what are you d——' The words died away and a look of horror crept across the face of the night duty sister as they emerged into the open space by the desk and the full realisation of what was occurring hit her.

'Tell her to open the cupboard and get the drugs,' the panting voice muttered in her ear, jabbing whatever it was into her back as she shrank away from his breath.

'She can't do that without two sets of keys. Come through and sit in here while she finds them.' Elly was surprised to hear how calm her voice sounded.

Would it work? she wondered. At the moment, it was imperative to her that she get the man out of the main corridor where other people might trigger off more madness, and into a position where the ward full of patients could remain undisturbed.

'I've a gun in her back and I'll shoot her if I have to,' he said to the bemused sister, 'so hurry yourself.'

A surge of thankfulness flooded through Elly when she realised he was actually pushing her towards the open door of the interview-room. The night sister would call security who would contact the police, and the emergency procedures that the hospital had in place for this type of situation would slide into action. She tried not to think about the efficiency or otherwise of Ted Eames, then remembered that the night security was a different man.

She tried to recall the order of the events that would be taking place outside at this moment, but her mind had blurred.

'Sit over there,' he ordered.

She did exactly as he had told her, sitting down to face the man, and his gun. Part of her was relieved to be free of his rough handling, but the sight of the gun was almost too stark a reality. He pushed the door shut and sank into the chair opposite her with the relief of a person who had reached a resting place just in time.

He looked so young, and very frightened! Grubby and unkempt, as if he lived in refuse bins like street kids she'd seen on television. He was shaking more than she was, and in a detached way, she noted his runny nose, and almost uncontrollable yawning. As he knuckled his free hand first into one eye, then the other, the symptoms of drug withdrawal, written on a blackboard during her training, flashed vividly into her mind.

She tried to remember how long since the last dose these symptoms would appear, then decided that wasn't terribly important. What she should be trying to remember was the next stage of withdrawal.

Through the closed door she could hear bustling activity, and she knew she had to talk to keep his attention off what might be going on in the corridor.

'Would you like something to eat or drink? I could ring through to the kitchens.'

'Keep away from the phone,' he warned. 'We won't be here long enough to worry about food. Your mate should have the cupboard open by now. I don't need much!'

His voice, pitched high and cracking, as if under some intolerable strain, still held a desperate plea for understanding. He wants me to like him, Elly realised in amazement.

'It may take longer than you think,' she said placatingly, and was rewarded by a stream of vicious epithets that made her mouth go dry with a sudden fear. This was real, not make-believe, she warned herself, and the young man was as volatile as a lit fuse.

Across the little room, her captor watched the door although his head whipped back towards her every time she made the slightest movement. Outside, she heard a hasty murmur and the sound of scuffling feet, then the shrill ringing of the phone diverted her attention, and her hand reached out automatically to pick it up.

'Don't touch it,' her captor barked, and she shrank back into her chair, while the jangling insistence dragged across her raw nerves until she wanted to scream.

'Pick it up and tell them to hurry—nothing else mind,' he said, when he could obviously stand it no longer.

Elly lifted the receiver.

'Sister Winthrop here,' she said with mechanical efficiency, and heard a male voice introduce himself as police and urge her to sit tight and not panic.

'He only wants pethidine,' she heard her own voice saying calmly, 'and could you please hurry?'

'If anyone comes in, be prepared to drop to the floor and stay there,' the voice said.

'Hang the thing up now!' the youth yelled, half rising

out of his chair, and waving the gun about dangerously.

'They're coming with the drug,' she told him, and hoped that what she said was true, then wondered, stupidly, if Mrs Hobson had got her message, and if her brothers knew their father was dead. They'd come up for the funeral, of course, her mind decided. Would they want to organise it? What would her father have wanted?

She looked at the boy, who appeared so uncared for, and remembered the man who had cared for her, who had to taught her to laugh in the face of danger, and stand square on to trouble whenever and wherever she encountered it, and hot slow tears slid down her cheeks.

Now the boy was screaming at her, telling her not to cry! Begging her not to cry or he would have to hit her. He lunged out of his chair towards her, the gun upraised above his head, his screams rising higher and higher, mingling with a wild pandemonium outside the door. Then the lights went out and there was a lot of noise and she forgot about dropping to the floor.

She woke to a room filled with red roses, yet heavy with the scent of narcissus and jonquils and other special flowers of spring. Turning her head to look out the window, she saw the vase of delicate blooms on the table by her bed, but the roses assaulted her eyes and reminded her of death and funerals.

'Is my father dead?' she asked, somehow hoping it might be a dream.

'Yes, Elly,' a deep, dark voice said, and she turned to see Gregor Ballantyne sitting by the bed, his eyes red-rimmed in a face so drawn and tired he looked like a smudged photo of the man she remembered.

'Not at the hospital!' she said, an instant spurt of

panic she could not understand fluttering in her chest. 'You promised!'

'I don't think I can keep that promise,' he said, with a desperation she recognised but couldn't understand.

'You must, you must,' she insisted fractiously, although she didn't know why she was so upset.

'Then I'll go now,' he said, dropping the words like cold stones on to her body as he rose and stood above her like a marble statue, his face a mask of dreadful sorrow. 'Now that I know you're OK!'

And he turned his back and walked out the door, leaving her feeling alone and sick and suddenly bereft.

Time lost all meaning as she lay, first in the hospital bed, and later in the sunny guest room of her brother's house in Sydney, her thoughts like the fractured images in a kaleidoscope, twisting and turning in a myriad patterns but not making a complete picture of anything.

People told her facts, repeating them in answer to her persistent questioning. Her father had died. She'd missed the funeral. She'd been hit on the head by a crazy young kid looking for drugs, and the second knock in such a short time had resulted in serious concussion for which she had been hospitalised.

Now released and swept south by the new head of the family, she was being watched and cosseted and loved and fussed over, and felt so unhappy that she cried most of the time.

'I think I'll go home and go back to work,' she told her sister-in-law, Nancy, as she mopped at eyes red from weeping. 'At least if I'm doing something, I'll have to make an effort to stop this nonsense.'

'You're suffering all the classic symptoms of post-traumatic stress disorder, probably with a bit of post-concussional syndrome thrown in,' replied the competent physician who had married her brother. 'As far as the stress is concerned, it could be exacerbated by returning to the place where the trauma occurred. After bank robberies, they usually switch staff around, change their jobs, look for alternatives that don't constantly remind those affected of what happened.'

'I can't even remember all that happening so how can it be affecting me like this?' she cried. 'And what else can a nurse do?'

'Nurse somewhere else, like here, for instance. Or go back to the study and research you gave up when you decided to go and live with Dad.'

'I was doing some research at Gracemere,' she said casually, then saw, in a flash of memory as clear as a film clip, Gregor Ballantyne sitting across the desk from her, his head bent over her file.

I have no claim on him, she reminded the self that was suddenly shot through with pain.

'Someone else will continue that,' Nancy assured her, 'although we know the hospital will hold your position open for you until you decide whether you want to return. The phone calls from that place are constant!'

Elly nodded. She'd tried to talk to people last week, but any voice from that part of her life reduced her mind to chaos again. She'd seen the lists that Nancy kept, noting down the caller and the message each time, seen Sue's name and Sally's, Grant's and Maggie's, even Clive's, but the one name she wanted to see was not there.

'I've got to go home some time,' she said feebly to Nancy. 'I'm over the dizziness and nausea that the concussion brought on, it's only my mind that's still fuzzy. Maybe, if I'm at home, it will click back into gear and the world of reality will return.'

'It might work that way,' her sister-in-law replied doubtfully, 'and Mrs Hobson is there. . .'

'I don't need a carer, Nancy!' she retorted.

'Don't you?'

Something in Nancy's voice pierced the thick fog of depression that had hung about her for weeks.

'You think I do?'

'I think you probably need professional help from a good psychologist. I think there's more than Dad's death and the episode with the young druggie, traumatic though both of those might be, behind all this welter of tears and self-pity.'

'Do you think that's all it is—self-pity?' she asked, stung by the acerbity in the measured words.

'I think it's a large part of it,' Nancy confirmed. 'I'll allow you the post-everything syndromes, Elly, but you're tougher than that. You're a fighter, and you're not fighting! Something's knocked the stuffing out of you, something's happened to make you want to hide away down here, rather than go back up there and face whatever it is that's bothering you.'

'I don't think "knocked the stuffing out of you" is an accepted clinical diagnosis, doctor dear,' Elly replied with a wry grin, hiding the pain that Nancy's insight had caused. 'But I do agree that home's the place I've got to go if I'm ever to sort myself out. I thought you were arguing against it?'

'I was, if you were only going home to be miserable there,' Nancy told her. 'If you go back for a positive reason, to pack up and move on, to find a new job, to actually get on with your life, then I'll sort out your brothers, who'll both cluck and wave their arms in the air, and I'll cheer you on.'

They were sitting in the living-room, looking out

over a garden alive with spring colour, with jonquils and narcissus under the trees, and azaleas rioting down the drive. There'd been jonquils and narcissus at the hospital, she remembered, when Gregor was there.

When Gregor was there! He *had* been there! Shock stopped the breath in her lungs, and it was only after she'd regained control that she could turn to Nancy.

'Were you there while I was in hospital?' she asked, hoping the query sounded sufficiently casual to not alert this percipient woman to anything untoward.

'We flew up early the morning after Dad died. You were out cold for three or four days, I'm not quite sure how long, but I know Bill nearly went berserk when he heard what had happened, and wanted you whipped away to another hospital.'

'But I wasn't moved, was I?' She looked back over at the garden, while in her mind, she could smell the special fragrance of the narcissus.

'No way!' Nancy assured her. 'Bill met his match in that chap who owned the hospital. He hovered over you like an angry bull, refusing to leave your room, would you believe, until you'd regained consciousness and he was certain you were going to be all right?'

Did that make it better or worse? she wondered, as a strange mixture of sadness and gladness filtered through her body.

'I thought I remembered seeing him there,' she said, with a careful lack of emphasis.

'Probably worried about a compensation claim, Bill reckoned,' Nancy added, and Elly had to smile.

'I accused him of that myself once,' she said, and was pleased she could remember.

'Well, if you want my opinion, he was too upset for it to be purely business,' Nancy replied, but Elly was not going to be drawn. Her day out with Gregor

Ballantyne and his subsequent visit to her home had taken on the substance of a dream, and part of her grieved for a loss she could not understand, because it was for something she had never had.

The idea stirred through her cloudy mind, lighting up dark corners, and found a question. Was she hiding down here from Gregor, or from the fact that there would be no Gregor in her life?

'I'll go home,' she said, knowing the answer wasn't here. 'Let's find a flight and ring the Hobsons and get me started before Bill comes home and wants to argue. I've got to get myself back on track, and no one but me can do it!'

'Bravo!' Nancy acclaimed. 'Now I know you're going to be OK. But promise me you'll seek professional help if you can't sort it out alone. And to prove you can manage on your own, why don't you phone an airline and arrange your own flight? That way, I won't be telling my husband lies when I say I couldn't stop you.'

Elly laughed, and decided that the sound was good. The calendar by the phone read the twentieth of September and, while she waited in a queue to be answered, she worked out that it must be five weeks since her father's death—five weeks out of her life that she would remember only in snatches.

'Can we make the airport in an hour?' she called to Nancy, confirming her booking when she heard a yell of agreement.

'The flight arrives at two-fifteen,' she told a delighted Mrs Hobson, and felt a pang of anger with herself for letting the situation drift for as long as it had. She was happy for the Hobsons to stay on in the downstairs flat forever, but what if they had wanted to leave, to get on with their own lives, while she had lain around like a zombie, refusing to take any action, or make a single decision?

But that anger was also good, she decided quite rationally as she hurried from the phone to pack her belongings. It was as if, with her decision to return home made, her feelings were once again registering in her mind. Which was what she wanted, wasn't it?

CHAPTER TEN

HAD the Gold Coast always looked this clean and bright? she wondered as they drove up the highway from the airport towards her home. The buildings seemed to sparkle in the bright light, and the sun, biting into her skin through the car window, was like a benediction.

'What's that about the electricity?' she asked, realising she'd missed a whole segment of Mrs Hobson's conversation while she looked about with the simple wonder of a child.

'I know the account came, but Bill said it wasn't with the mail we re-addressed down to you in Sydney. I seem to think it was earlier than that—while you were in hospital perhaps.'

'Did we get cut off?' she asked, idiotically pleased to be bothered about something so simple as an electricity account.

'No, they rang to see if there was a problem, and agreed to wait until you got back although Hobson offered to pay it.'

Mr Hobson, who had never shown objection to his wife's use of his surname, merely nodded his agreement and concentrated on the traffic.

'I'll fix it up as soon as we get home,' Elly assured them both.

'If we find the letter,' Mrs Hobson said in a voice filled with dismay that some detail of her duty might have been neglected. It was as if, having remembered, she must pursue the thought to a satisfactory conclusion.

171

'I'm certain the company will be delighted to tell me how much we owe,' Elly said, slipping back into her familiar role as ultimate authority.

'But there might have been other letters with it,' Mrs Hobson argued, and Elly changed the subject by asking about rain, and Mr Hobson's lawn bowls, then sat back in her seat and listened to the chatter with a feeling that perhaps she could survive after all.

The sadness she'd expected to feel with the knowledge that her father was no longer waiting for her in the house did not come, and instead there was such a warm familiarity about her home that, it was as if he were back as she had known him before his illness. He had never been obtrusive in her life, guiding her more than pushing her when she was young, and later offering support when she needed it, advice if she asked. She realised that he had left enough of himself with her to still provide that guidance and advice, and had surely brought her up strong enough to support herself.

A squat vase filled with freesias scented the rooms, welcoming her back, and she thought of Alexander and the red roses that had followed her to Sydney, and the letter she'd forced herself to write, telling him she couldn't accept them. Had she been too hasty? Maybe an Alexander was just what she needed in her life for a while.

Then Franny was there, winding round her ankles, complaining vociferously about her prolonged absence and demanding attention.

When the phone rang, she picked up the receiver absentmindedly, her hand automatically obeying the strident summons.

'I was ringing to ask for a progress report from Mrs Hobson,' Sue said delightedly, 'but as you're back, I'll get organised and call in on my way to work to see you for myself.'

Elly nodded and smiled. Useless to argue with Sue, and a bit of hospital news might help her decide whether she wanted to go back to Gracemere or look for something else to fill her days and occupy her mind. She pushed the thoughts of Gregor away. Sue would fill her in on what was happening and part of what was happening would surely include the new owner—but she wouldn't ask, she warned herself, as her stomach squeezed itself into a little ball and her determination wavered ever so slightly.

Sue brought her vivacity into the room, making Elly feel more alive than she had in weeks. Together they dissected Elly's replacement in Neurovascular—'a temporary appointment, as we all keep pointing out to the poor woman'—the surgical staff, the new crop of nurse graduates and finally Administration.

'Of course the new owner is no longer with us,' Sue said chattily. 'Once he'd got the place running his way, he was off to bigger challenges.'

'Doing what?' Elly asked, hoping she didn't sound overly interested.

'I'm not certain. Word is he's gone back to Melbourne. The business with that young addict——' Elly saw the keenness in her glance '—really threw him. He hovered by your bedside as if he'd been personally responsible for putting your life in danger, in spite of the fact that the security in the place had been set up by the previous owners. You'll be pleased to know it's all been tightened.'

'But how can it be, with people coming in and going out at all hours?'

'He's put security staff in the front entrance and in A and E, and closed off the car park. We can only get in and out with a special card issued to all staff.'

'And what about the visitor who comes in during the day, and waits down in the car park till evening?' Elly asked, unsettled enough by the news of Gregor's absence to want to find holes in his scheme.

'The door from the car park into the hospital is worked on the same card. In and out, would you believe?'

'And what happens if you lose your card, or in the case of fire? I can just see us all pushing cards into doors in a frantic effort to evacuate the place.'

'I might have known your mind would think of that, while we all accepted thankfully that someone was looking after our welfare!' Sue grumbled. 'If you lose your card, there's a buzzer that will call up security staff, and if ever there's a fire, the circuit which controls all the door locks cuts out automatically as soon as the alarm sounds and the sprinklers come on.'

'Brilliant,' Elly decreed, but could not refrain from adding, 'and, having locked you all safely inside his hospital, he departs?'

'Well, with a good administration, there really wouldn't be a job for him here, now would there?' Sue asked, as if making excuses for his absence.

The conversation drifted back to people they knew and rested easily there until it was time for Sue to leave.

'Lovely flowers,' she said, as she walked to the stairs, and Elly looked at them absentmindedly.

'I suppose Mrs Hobson bought them,' she told Sue, following her down and out to her car, her body drinking in the warmth of the sun.

'Will you come back?' Sue asked, casually, but Elly knew it was the most important question of the afternoon.

'I don't know, Sue,' she replied, honestly acknowledging that she'd had no sudden revelations about her future since her arrival home. She watched her friend drive away, envying her the sense of purpose she knew was lacking in her own life.

'There were two or three letters together, came in the post the day your father died. I remember that part now. I was coming through here when Hobson called out to me, and I put them down somewhere,' Mrs Hobson was saying as she walked back inside and encountered the housekeeper hovering in the entry.

'It doesn't matter, Mrs Hobson,' Elly assured her. 'I'll ring the electricity company right now, and send them a cheque this afternoon.'

'I know it doesn't matter, but I don't want to start losing things just yet. It'll be bad enough later on, if I get like your poor father, but I'm not ready yet.'

She fussed away, trying to retrace a path she'd taken five weeks earlier, before the house had been thrown into an uproar with the arrival of nine more Winthrops, all of whom had squeezed in to the old holiday home.

'Thank you for the flowers,' Elly called after her, catching the scent of them once again as she walked up the stairs.

She heard a muttered reply and smiled. Mrs Hobson prided herself on her efficiency, and Elly knew the housekeeper wouldn't rest until this one small lapse had been rectified.

So Gregor Ballantyne had gone away, she told herself, her fingers brushing the petals of the fragrant flowers. Did that make the decision to return to work easier or harder?

Had he told her he was going while she was in hospital? She tried to remember if they'd had any conversations, but only had the haziest recollection of his being there, and she wasn't certain whether she actually remembered, or knew from people telling her.

She woke to sun streaming through the window, and a certainty that she had slept deeply and soundly. Mrs Hobson had cooked dinner for her and packed her off to bed early the previous night, correctly diagnosing a return to the teary Elly as over-tiredness after the long day.

She half remembered a quotation she'd once heard, about each new day being the beginning of the rest of one's life, and thought of the conversations she'd had about new beginnings, and new directions. She was no longer tied up at a crossroads—except in her mind!

'They were in the yellow pages of the phone book downstairs,' Mrs Hobson announced triumphantly climbing up the stairs with unusual vigour. 'The electricity bill and one other. I must have put them down on the phone table, then used them to mark a place in the book later on. It was put away and that was that.'

She came out on to the veranda, where Elly was sitting in her favourite chair enjoying a cup of tea, Franny purring contentedly in her lap. With a flourish that told of her delight in finding them, she passed the letters to Elly, the top one a window-fronted account, and the second addressed to herself, in strong black handwriting that was unfamiliar.

'Thanks, Mrs Hobson,' she said with a smile, and went on to assure her that she would look after herself for meals from now on. 'It's time I got back to normality,' she told her. 'And shopping is about as normal as you can get!'

When Mrs Hobson had gone, she turned the letter over in her hands and tested its weight, feeling a bulky heaviness. The envelope was a thick creamy bond, good quality paper, with a Melbourne address she didn't recognise on the back of it.

A faint ray of hope crept through her, until she remembered that this letter had arrived weeks ago, and Gregor had only recently left for Melbourne. Who had written it and why? She held it in her hand, like a present she didn't want to open in case she was disappointed with the contents.

'Shall we go and sit outside, Fran?' she asked the cat, and, correctly assuming she'd be followed, she walked down the stairs and out the front door, crossing the road to sit at the picnic table under the tall Norfolk pines.

The envelope refused to reveal its secret, so, with fingers slowed by reluctance, she pulled up the flap and withdrew three pages of matching creamy paper, covered with the same heavy script.

The date was the day before her father had died, the signature Gregor's! Her heart gave one gigantic leap, then sank like a stone in her chest. He'd written to say he'd made a mistake, that's why she hadn't seen him or heard from him since she regained consciousness in hospital. That must be it! Why else would he have written when she'd seen him the same morning?

She squashed the unread pages in her hands, and the nausea of recent weeks returned in an all-encompassing wave. Around her, the air was alive with the special magic of spring, the bright shining freshness that touched the grass and trees and water to new life, yet she felt as dead as her father.

'Do you really believe there are no ends, but only new beginnings?'

She heard his voice as clearly as if he was sitting beside her, and knew she had to read the letter. Had to have an end, before she could gather up the pieces of her life and begin again—today or any other day!

'Dear Elly,' he had written. She took a deep breath and her eyes slid down the page.

I have thought of nothing but you since we parted, and even now my twisting mind will not allow me to rest. Two nights without sleep will render me a complete idiot and the work I hoped to achieve while down here will be useless. Maybe, if I say what is in my heart, I will be able to relax, and, although I fear it might frighten you away, I believe it must be said.

My problem is, dear Elly, that I fear I'll not be able to keep to our agreement. I did not ask you to marry me to get you into my bed, but because, by some strange alchemy, you have turned my life upside down, and a feeling I can only assume is love, has shattered my confidence and returned me to a bumbling adolescent state of sheer uncertainty I can't remember ever experiencing before. And you ask me to keep my feelings a secret in the hospital; to not smile when I see you behind your desk, so stiff and starchy in your immaculate white uniform! I fear you ask too much!

Can I stop my heart from beating faster, can I stop my lungs from dragging in deep gulps of air, and my hands from shaking with a need to reach out and touch you, hold you, draw you nearer to me? I cannot promise this!

I'll undertake to give you time, to try to keep a decent distance while you learn to know me, and perhaps to like me, but I can promise nothing, because every fibre in my being cries out for you, and this new distraction, this wholly unexpected madness, seems to be beyond any rational control.

Is it love, Elly? If it is, then love is new to me, and most uncomfortable, for I am a sane and sensible man who has, in recent years, guided his life by intellect not emotion, and am now in real danger of losing control.

The signature was scrawled across the page, and she could see where the nib of the pen had bitten into the paper, as if a strong emotion, akin to anger, had driven the word.

Her fingers smoothed the paper, running over and over the surface as if to absorb his words through her fingertips.

He'd said he loved her—if what he felt was love— yet now had gone away. No note, no phone call, no nothing!

She looked back at the words. They weren't the end she needed! Then she knew that she must speak to him.

'I don't know where he is,' she whispered to Franny, then remembered putting a slip of paper into her pocket. She couldn't be certain, but something told her it was a phone number, that he had rung her at work, and given it to her, that he'd wanted her to call him back, after—— The memory hit the thick blankness.

'The uniform you were wearing that dreadful night was thrown away,' Mrs Hobson told her. 'Covered in blood, they said it was!'

'Scalp wounds do bleed freely,' she responded absentmindedly as she walked up the stairs.

She could ring Gracemere and ask if they had a Melbourne number for him. No, that didn't seem right.

Would a phone call do? She rather thought not. If it was to be an end, it had to be achieved face to face.

She'd never been to Melbourne. Could she think of it as a holiday?

The idea of a holiday lent an added impetus to her movements, and two hours later, Mr and Mrs Hobson were driving her back to the airport, one in stoic silence, the other chattering cheerfully about what a good idea a holiday was, and what would she do about the flowers.

Mr Hobson was negotiating the traffic turning into the airport, and Elly pointed out which airline she was travelling, so it was only after they had checked her small suitcase and she was about to walk through the security grille into the departure lounge that she asked, 'What flowers?'

'The ones that come every second day. Narcissus and daffodils, freesias yesterday.'

'But I wrote to Alexander. . .'

'Hardly him,' Mrs Hobson said, shaking her head in dismissal of his thwarted suit. 'Not flashy enough for the likes of him.'

'Did you ring the florist and explain I was away and that they should stop sending them?' she asked, puzzled that Mrs Hobson's usual common sense had apparently deserted her.

'Of course I did. They must have contacted their client, and rang back to say the person who had ordered them said you'd be home one day, and they'd be there to welcome you when you finally arrived.'

They called her flight and she walked away, a part of her mind puzzling over the flowers, but her stomach already knotting anxiously at the thought of what might lie ahead.

Thirty-six Yelland Street was a large sprawling brick home set back from the street in an old well-established

garden, now alive with colour from banks of rhododen-
drons. Elly walked up the drive in the early dusk,
apprehension tugging at her feet, urging her to turn
around, to back away before it was too late.

'I'm sorry to bother you,' she said to the dark-haired
woman who answered the door. 'My name is Ellen
Winthrop and I'm trying to contact Gregor Ballantyne.
I had this address from his previous visit to
Melbourne.'

Her stomach was churning again, and her heart
thumped so loudly she was certain the woman must
hear it.

'He's staying here but he's not in at the moment,'
the woman said, and Elly heard a barely restrained
anger in her tone. Dear heaven, was the woman a
lover? Unlikely, if he'd written such a letter to her,
Elly, from this house!

'Could you tell me where I might be able to reach
him, or when it might be convenient to call?' she asked,
hoping she didn't sound as desperate as she felt. The
cab driver who had picked her up at the airport, after
hearing the address, had taken her to an elegant bed-
and-breakfast place only two streets away, but she was
uncertain she'd be able to force her legs to make the
walk a second time!

'If you're who I think you are, I'm not certain I
should tell you. He's been most upset,' the woman
said in a particularly proprietorial way that reminded
Elly of her brothers. 'Tell me where you're staying
and I'll let him know.'

Elly looked despairingly at the woman's shuttered
face and wondered if she would pass on a message.

'I have to see him,' she said, but the woman's lips
only tightened to a thinner, straighter line, and
Elly knew that a message wouldn't do.

'I'm sorry to have bothered you,' she said quietly, and turned away, walking down the drive, her head held high, stubborn pride and dogged determination both firmly in place.

I'll sit outside the front gate all night, she promised herself, knowing now that she had done the right thing in coming.

The headlights, already on in the dusky twilight, warned her of a car sweeping in, but she didn't recognise the Lexus until it skidded to a halt beside her and a joyous shout of 'Elly' split the air. Then she was swept into a tight embrace, and Gregor was holding her as if he would never let her go, murmuring her name over and over and over again.

'You wouldn't have come if you didn't want me, would you?' he asked at last, in a voice so rough with emotion it crawled over her skin and prickled wherever it touched. 'You wouldn't have come to say goodbye, Elly?'

She shook her head, unable to speak for the lump that blocked her throat completely.

Then his arms released her just enough for his head to drop down and his lips to meet hers, in a silent pledge of such magnitude that she felt the stupid tears sliding down her cheeks, touching their lips with the warm saltiness.

'Mrs Hobson lost your letter,' she said some time later, as if that simple statement might explain her being in the drive at thirty-six Yelland Street this late afternoon. 'I didn't read it till this morning.'

The words seem to penetrate some trance he'd departed into, and he pushed her back so he could peer down into her face.

'The letter I wrote from Melbourne last time I was down here?'

She had to smile at the incredulous tone of his voice, and at the bewildered shake of his head. Reaching up, she touched his cheek. 'It wasn't sent on to Sydney with the other mail, and it was only because the electricity account was lost with it that poor Mrs Hobson remembered that mail had come that day.'

His arms tightened around her, as if the memories of that time were almost beyond bearing.

'I didn't remember much for a long time,' she told him. 'Bits and pieces here and there, but nothing concrete.' She hesitated, not knowing how to continue, but certain that she must explain her torment. 'I didn't hear from you, and I didn't know if we . . .if anything. . .'

'Oh, Elly darling!' he murmured, squeezing the last bit of air from her lungs. 'My poor confused little love! Didn't know if we were already lovers? If anything existed between us?' he suggested.

'Didn't know if I should have heard from you, if I had any right to be expecting you to phone me, or come and see me. I wanted you so badly, but couldn't work out why or what had happened, and if you did care, why you hadn't come.'

She mumbled the words against his chest, ashamed of her own inadequacy, now that she was here with him.

'But you sent me away,' he told her, shaking her now as if willing her to remember. 'Told me I had to keep the promise!'

She shook her head, unable to remember such rash words.

'I was upsetting you so much, I thought I'd better go, but I hoped, once you were well enough and read the letter, that you'd contact me. . .'

'And I didn't get the letter!' she said, filled again

with the aching sadness that had characterised the last few weeks.

'Yes, you did,' he told her, shaking her again, but gently now, like a mother admonishing a child with loving kindness in the touch and and an infinite depth of feeling in the words. 'You read it today, and now you're here. Do you think that doesn't tell me something, my love, even if your head is still too confused to work it out.'

He rocked her against his body, and she drew strength from his warmth and firmness, melding her body against his until it seemed as if they were one.

His lips touched her hair and against her chest his lungs expanded as if he was breathing in her spirit.

'Are you well enough to be jaunting about like this?' he asked at last. 'You could have phoned, you know!'

The tightening of his arms belied this statement, and she chuckled.

'All I had was this address from that old letter,' she explained.

'You could have phoned the hospital. They have been under strict orders to contact me immediately if you rang.'

'I thought. . .' She battled to find the words she needed to explain her consternation. 'I decided. . .I had to know. . .I had to see you!' she finished finally, the inability to explain shrivelling her composure to a limp doubt.

'How can I reassure you?' he teased, looking into her face again with eyes so warm and soft and full of love that her mind went blank and her body started to shake with a need that fired her blood to a frenzied madness.

'Not here, I think,' he added with a strange smile, and she saw a matching passion flare in his eyes, and felt the yearning hunger in his hands now moving searchingly, insistently over her back. 'You'd better come inside and meet my sister Pam—she's Debbie Morrison's mother—while I explain I won't be home tonight.'

Several things clicked into place in Elly's mind as she remembered Debbie's mum's condemnation of Jocee, and understood the woman's reaction to herself.

But behind Gregor's casual words she had heard a shadow of doubt, and an echo of the pain he'd suffered, and still felt, because of it. She struggled to find words that might reassure him, but her own inexperience, her concern over arriving back at the bed-and-breakfast place with a man in tow—all the stupid practical details threw her mind into a panic again.

'Couldn't we just go to a hotel and phone from there to let them know where we are.'

She felt a movement ripple through him and knew that he was laughing at her.

'Without a piece of luggage, a toothbrush or a change of undies? Why not, my love? We'll do exactly that, and, if we choose an expensive enough hotel, it will have toothbrushes in the bathroom, and a bathrobe for each of us, should we feel any necessity to be clothed when room service brings us food.'

He let go of her, and reached out to open the car door, helping her in then bending to whisper in her ear, 'I love you, Elly Winthrop,' before he slammed the door and walked around the bonnet to slide behind the wheel.

So now she was committed, and a sense of peace slid through her, not deadening the excited anticipation of her body, but sharpening it, adding an extra dimension, like exotic spices added to a special meal.

Gregor's tension matched hers, as they drove in

silence towards the heart of the city. She could almost read the pulsing messages radiating from his body, and finally said in a small and quavering voice that was only half joking, 'Do you think we'll make it through the check-in procedures and get up to our room in time?'

'Only with a superhuman effort,' he replied, his voice a husky growl. 'The urge to pull this car over into a side street and ravish you in full view of any passer-by is almost overwhelming, but you deserve better than that, my sweet one—and so do I for putting up with the torture of the last five weeks. We are going to make love for the first time, slowly, and sensuously, and in as much comfort as I can arrange at such short notice.'

He was right about the comfort, Elly acknowledged, waking next morning to the sight of the city of Melbourne stretched beyond the wide windows of the suite. And sensuously? Well, she admitted to herself, sliding her hand over skin that was burning just thinking about the previous night, yes, that had been there.

But slowly? The heat crept to her cheeks as she remembered, in far too vivid detail, their arrival at the hotel. Once in their suite, she had been pushed towards the bathroom, while Gregor phoned his sister, and the bed-and-breakfast hostess, then ordered champagne and food and flowers—jonquils and narcissus and freesias that told her who had been sending the flowers to welcome her home!

Emerging, steaming slightly from the shower, damp ends of her hair clinging to her neck and shoulders, she'd seen him come into the bathroom behind her, and heard the long deep groan as he reached out and drew her against his body.

'Slowly' had been forgotten as their matching needs

met in a collision of such force that she had to shake her head at the memory, unable to believe the primal force that exploded between them even now, so many hours later.

At first it had been an awkward, uncomfortable, urgent jostling and scrambling to get his clothes off so their skin could slide together, learning the secrets of each other through all the tactile pleasure of fired-to-fever-pitch nerve-endings. Then other senses had come into play as she smelt his maleness and her own body responded with a sudden film of perspiration, that he licked at, sucked, and tasted, tongue probing and stroking, teasing and tantalising, sending her into an agony of wanting that threatened to erupt again and again, as they found their own uniqueness in the matching of their bodies—limbs and angles, bones and skin and sinews—fitting together at last like two parts of a whole, so the final frenzied act of love made them one in such a cataclysm of feeling that Elly wondered if it could ever be the same again.

It had been the same again!

She smiled in wonder. The same only so much sweeter, and more satisfying, and unbelievably erotic. Her thoughts brought her nipples to peaking buds again and the tingling, throbbing, aching urgency in the soft mound between her legs made her wonder, with a dazed concern, if she might be a nymphomaniac. Could she possibly want more sex?

Then Gregor turned, still half asleep, and one heavy arm reached out and drew her close, and she felt his body's leaping response to hers, and wondered what a male nymphomaniac was called.

It was her last conscious thought for some time, until, sated by a climactic release that sent her spinning out into another dimension, to return reluctantly to earth in Gregor's arms, she heard him pledge himself to her.

'I love you, and need you, and want you by my side forever, Sister Winthrop, my Elly, my darling, my own true love! Will you marry me?'

And this time she didn't argue, or make conditions, or even reply, but the kiss she pressed on his lips, and the light he saw shining in her clear green eyes, told him more than any words could ever have conveyed, and he folded her against his body and held her close, free at last from the doubts and confusion he had felt from the first moment he saw her.

Look out for Temptation's bright, new, stylish covers...

They're Terrifically Tempting!

We're sure you'll love the new raspberry-coloured Temptation books—our brand new look from December.

Temptation romances are still as passionate and fun-loving as ever and they're on sale now!

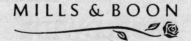

MILLS & BOON

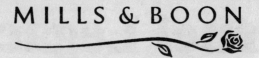

MILLS & BOON